MW01234018

Let Sleeping Dogs Lie

Murder Most Mysterious, Volume 1

Janice Alonso

Published by Janice Alonso, 2020.

This is a work of fiction. Similarities to real people, places, or events are entirely coincidental.

LET SLEEPING DOGS LIE

First edition. August 5, 2020.

ISBN: 979-8224686650

Written by Janice Alonso.

Let Sleeping Dogs Lie
By Janice Alonso

Chapter One

"**D**oes the expression 'Rode hard and put away wet' mean anythin' to you?" Using her few good teeth, Blythe Rawlins gnawed the end of the toothpick, tonguing the splinters into a little ball, and spit it toward the floor. The wad landed on the toe of Coqui's boot.

Grabbing a grainy, brown napkin from a metal dispenser, Coqui leaned over and wiped away the glob. Straightening, she smiled and answered, "I'm familiar with the expression."

"That best described Earlene Thornton. She was one of them women born to be used. No surprise when she was charged with murder." Blythe turned up the bottle and polished off what was left of the beer. "All that abuse buildin' up inside her had to come out one day."

A flash of lightning danced across the crone's face, illuminating the vertical lines racing toward her mouth, lines etched from a lifetime of a hot and heavy relationship with cigarettes and booze. According to the smell drifting across the table from her clothes and breath, they were still on intimate terms.

Rain pelted the windows, sending drops squiggling down the panes. Their table was in the far corner of Cooter's Rough 'n Tumble. The Saturday night crowd created a noisy and suffocating atmosphere. Cooter's was the kind of place where there was only one table reserved for nonsmokers; most nights, that was one table too many.

1

"What'd you say your name was again, missy?" The old woman snorted and then a crackle of laughter erased what was left of the smile on Coqui's face.

"Coqui . . . Coqui Jones."

"Coqui?" Blythe's face bunched into folds of confusion, causing the wrinkles to sink deeper. The woman wore her pewter-gray hair cropped close to the head, and several jet-black whiskers sprouted from her chin. One gnarly hand wrapped around the beer bottle while the other one stroked it like it was a beloved pet.

"Puerto Rican tree frog," Coqui answered. She didn't add that the reason for her name was because she was the result of her parents' weekend honeymoon in San Juan. Coqui remained the only child of the Harlem wild child who'd met his Georgia bride on a community service trip to Jamaica for a small infraction during his freshman year in college. Coqui's mom and her parents had been in the same village repairing the shack of a building the residents used as their church. Her grandfather had been a fire-and-brimstone preacher and his wife fanned those altruistic flames in their quest to promote peace and harmony in the world. It was love at first sight for Coqui's parents, and they were married two months after they returned from the mission trip.

Coqui pointed to the empty bottle. "Would you like another beer?" Blythe nodded. Since Coqui was here to gather as much information as she could about Earlene Thornton, she wanted to keep the old woman chatty.

Blythe's rheumy eyes settled on Coqui's face, her body swaying inward. "Why you so interested in Earlene? The murder was twenty-five years ago."

Coqui leaned inward and glided a business card across the table. Blythe's hand unfolded, picked up the card, and an arthritic finger traced its edges. Thunder rumbled as the rain's intensity mounted.

Blythe glanced at the card and with a flick of the wrist she tossed it back onto the table. "Still don't answer my question. What's your business with Earlene?" Her lips parted as a burp filled the space between them.

"Her daughter has asked me to reopen the file," said Coqui, leaning backward for a breath of better air.

"Julie Ann? I haven't seen her since her mama's trial . . . she was only eighteen."

Coqui did a mental tabulation . . . that would make Julie Ann forty-three. *Eleven years older than me*, thought Coqui.

Easing forward, Blythe lifted the bottle with both hands and placed her elbows on the table's edge. "I remember when Julie Ann was born like it was yesterday. Earlene was my second cousin. We was like this." She extended two nicotine-stained fingers, wiggling them side-by-side.

"We used to double date . . . Jack Thornton and Ricky Rawlins." She shook her head. "When Jack learned Earlene was pregnant, he was thrilled. We went out and had ourselves a double weddin'." Blythe frowned. "He got killed in a car wreck on Highway 54 the weekend after Thanksgiving, before Julie Ann was born."

"Let's get back to the murder," Coqui interrupted. "Julie Ann's the one who saw her mother standing over Dexter Sterling's body, the gun in her hand." When Blythe offered no comment, Coqui continued. "Earlene confessed to the murder."

"From Earlene's lips," confirmed Blythe, "to Chief Holbrook's ears."

"You got there right after Julie Ann screamed."

Blythe's eyes wouldn't meet Coqui's. "What about that beer?" Her tongue rolled across her lower lip.

Coqui signaled the waitress.

A trim blond woman, whose name tag identified her as Ruthie, set down a frosty, fresh bottle.

"Thanks," said Coqui. Then she returned her attention to Blythe. "Julie Ann thinks Earlene's innocent," she continued.

"She never did believe her mama murdered Dexter," said Blythe.

"Julie Ann's asked me to find the real killer."

Blythe swallowed hard. "Earlene's the real killer."

"Maybe she is; maybe she isn't." Coqui toyed with the cork coaster under her sparkling water.

"She's always had a bee in her bonnet about that trial. Earlene's always stopped her –"

"Her mama died last week," cut in Coqui.

Evidently, that was not news to Blythe. "That's what I hear," she mumbled. Leaning back, she said, "Well, Miss Private Investigator, dig away." She spread her hands and flashed a snaggle-toothed smile.

Coqui nodded and pulled out a small legal pad and pencil. "Julie Ann told me to start with you, Mrs. Rawlins, since you were the first one . . ." Coqui paused and met Blythe's intense gaze. "According to the reports . . . to arrive on the scene after Julie Ann's scream."

"I told Chief Holbrook everythin' then." Blythe shrugged. "Don't even know if I can recollect anythin'."

Coqui's lips thinned, tiring of their cat-and-mouse banter. "Try to remember."

Blythe's head tilted backward and rested on the curve of the padded seat. She closed her eyes. "Dexter Sterling." She sang out the name as if it were the opening number from a Broadway musical. Her eyes slit open, and her head lolled to one side, focusing her attention on Coqui. "Dexter was a looker if I ever saw one. He talked the panties off near every female in Lamar County." Her face sobered. "But he was as mean as a man could be. Don't know of a soul who mourned his passin'."

"Tell me more about Dexter," said Coqui.

"He was a drifter." The old woman pursed her lips. "He cruised into town one day drivin' a white Ninety-eight Oldsmobile convertible."

"When was this . . . that he arrived in Hampton?" interrupted Coqui.

Blythe shrugged. "The spring Earlene was a senior and I was a junior."

"1975?"

"Yup – 1975 graduating class of the Hampton Pirates."

"Dexter's first time to Hampton?"

Blythe nodded as she regained her train of thought. "A real charmer that Dexter. Had those dark looks that warn a woman to stand clear but finds herself snaked in anyway. Like all the other girls in town, me and Earlene knew who he was. Both of us had crushes on him, but we was goin' with Jack and Ricky." She paused. "Dexter stayed at an Alamo Plaza on the edge of town. Had a different woman every week. Chief Holbrook had to drive out there many times to break up the fussin' and fightin'. Then one night Dexter beat up a woman so bad, she ended up in the emergency room. The next mornin', he cruised right out of town just like he'd cruised in."

"He wasn't ever arrested?" asked Coqui.

"Nary a one filed a complaint. Then he showed up thirteen years later . . . that's when he started sniffin' around Earlene. For a while, I thought she'd tamed him. He stopped drinkin' and they started goin' to church. Then just as quick as he'd stopped, he went back to his old ways."

Blythe gulped more of the beer and then pointed the bottleneck in Coqui's direction. "He began poundin' on Earlene. One night he smacked her so hard across the face that she fell and broke both arms tryin' to cushion herself as she headed for the floor. She was in the hospital over a month."

A burst of raucous laughter drown out their conversation. Revelers had steadily filled the diner, and a cloud of thick smoke lay over the room. Most of the patrons of Cooter's came in groups of threes and fours, men settling in at the bar, women preferring the tables and booths. From what Coqui could tell, they left by twos, drunk, and in sloppy, wet lip-locks. Coqui massaged her temples, her head thickening with the promise of a migraine. She reached into her shoulder bag and rooted around until she came up with a bottle of aspirin. Popping two caplets in her mouth, she washed them down with the water.

Clearing her throat, Coqui looked back to Blythe, "What happened to Julie Ann while Earlene was in the hospital?"

Blythe flattened her shoulders against the back of the seat. "A woman named Brenda Watkins took her in. After the doctors released Earlene, Julie Ann went back home, but the Watkins took responsibility for their upkeep. Miss Brenda, that is." Blythe took a breath. "The Watkins was the richest family around and Brenda was their only child. She never married, and she took a special interest in Julie Ann, kinda like she was her own."

"How old was Julie Ann then?" Coqui asked. "When Brenda Watkins took her in?"

Her eyes squinted, trying to conjure up a memory. "'Bout twelve or thirteen I'd say. She was tall for her age – kinda gangly, not like her mama. Earlene always looked like a pixie to me, with that blonde hair and those big blue eyes." A slight smile wiggled to her lips. "Always neat as a pin, everythin' had its place, and everythin' was in its place."

Coqui thought about Julie Ann now. She was still much taller than most women but had added quite a bit of weight over the years. "And where was Dexter during this time?" asked Coqui.

"He skedaddled. Didn't come back until three days before he was murdered."

Coqui looked up from her notes. "He was gone for six years? And then he just appeared after all that time and was killed three days later?"

"He came and went as he pleased." Blythe's blinks became slower, with less open time in between. "Dexter had a knack for disappearin' when trouble came lookin' for him and poppin' back up after . . ." Her voice trailed off, and Coqui couldn't make out the last few words.

When Blythe didn't resume her story, Coqui shook her hand. "Mrs. Rawlins," she called softly, then a little louder over the drunken din. "Mrs. Rawlins."

Blythe's eyes opened and gazed at Coqui like she might remember her from some distant past. Coqui sighed and raised her hand for the waitress.

As Ruthie approached, a smile crossed her face. She tugged the sleeve of the old woman's gray cardigan. "Miss Blythe . . . Miss Blythe." She released her grip on the sweater. "That's all you're going to get from her tonight."

Coqui squeezed her eyes shut and pinched the bridge of her nose. Then she looked up at Ruthie and sighed. "Where does she live?"

"Out in the country in a little trailer park just south of here on the outskirts of Hampton."

Coqui looked at her phone: it was eleven-thirty. She glanced out the window. Water pooled into red clay puddles in the parking lot, rain dimpling their surfaces. If she took Blythe home and then drove all the way back to Atlanta where she lived, Coqui wouldn't be home until close to three. Maybe later in this weather. And she still didn't have the information she needed to begin her investigation. Coqui stared at the little creature hunkered over in the chair across from her. "Is there a place to stay the night?"

"Her, too?" asked Ruthie.

Coqui nodded.

"There's the Oak Tree Inn just down the road," said Ruthie. "I'll call to see if there's a vacancy."

Coqui smiled. "Thanks."

Chapter Two

The sounds of passing semis and car horns woke Coqui the following morning. Oak Tree Inn was nestled snuggly by I-75, the main drag to Florida and a convenient stop for an overnight stay. Stretching over to the nightstand, she tilted the phone in her direction: 7:00. She lifted her head higher and peered to the bed opposite her. Coqui had been fortunate to grab the last available room at Oak Tree Inn last night, even more fortunate that the accommodation had twin beds. Blythe's mouth gaped open, emitting little snoring puffs, and her chest rose and fell in a steady, rhythmic tempo. Coqui breathed in deeply, and her stomach lurched. She clamped a hand tightly to cover her mouth and nose. If possible, Blythe's smell had bumped up a couple of notches in the past few hours. Coqui raised her left arm and sniffed; she was beginning to smell as bad as her roomie.

Coqui crawled out of bed and snagged her clothes from the night before draped across the room's only chair. Grabbing her tote, she tiptoed into the bathroom and eased shut the door. A pine-scented disinfectant invaded her senses. Her hand traced the wall searching for the switch, and then she turned on the florescent overhead light. Coqui took in her surroundings. The Oak Tree Inn appeared to have been built and decorated in the seventies. While its avocado green appointments were dated, each nook and cranny was pristine.

Coqui gazed at her reflection. Removing a rubber band from a toiletry pouch, she gathered her black, corkscrew hair into a ponytail.

Her emerald green eyes were surrounded by a sea of red, compliments of the smoky air from the previous night. Her hair was a gift from her father's gene pool, the color of her eyes from her mother's. After studying herself in the mirror, she decided to save her shower for later and then scrubbed her face, brushed her teeth, and freshened up as best as she could.

Walking outside, Coqui made her way past the row of rooms after hers on her way toward the lobby. All the rooms were identical. Each had a large window next to its sole outside door and overlooked the parking lot. This morning, most of the doors sported "Do Not Disturb" signs hanging from their knobs.

The air was crisp and the trees around the inn displayed the deep oranges, yellows, and russets one would expect in late October in Georgia. A shroud of heavy dampness cloaked her shoulders even though the rain had stopped. The parking lot held a smattering of cars; crusted mud and large drops of water dotted their tires, hoods, windows, and roofs. It was Sunday morning, and all was still – a sharp contrast to the previous night.

When Coqui stepped on the outside mat leading into the entrance to the lobby, automatic double doors slid open. The woman behind the desk glanced up and smiled. She appeared to be in her mid-forties and wore a tan uniform with Oak Tree Inn embroidered across the left side of the bodice. Her name was Deborah.

"Sleep alright?" she asked.

"Just like home," said Coqui.

"The diner across the parking lot is open for breakfast. Harold makes mighty fine biscuits and red eye gravy, but if what you're after is coffee, it's set up over there by the fireplace." She extended an arm to the opposite side of the room. "*The Atlanta Journal-Constitution* is on the table between the sofas."

Coqui nodded. "Thanks"

"Just don't fill out the puzzle page," Deborah warned pleasantly, wagging her finger. "One of our housekeepers likes to tear it out and take it home to work on when she's done with her shift. She has a hissy-fit when somebody gets to it before her."

Coqui walked toward a Victorian buffet where two urns of coffee stood side-by-side, one identified as regular, the other as decaf. She placed an Atlanta Braves mug under the spout, and then moved over to the accompaniments. She frowned at the little packets of powdered milk and decided to pass.

Two chocolate-brown, vinyl sofas sat opposite each other with a small coffee table separating them, the promised newspaper spread across it. The grouping was in front of a stone fireplace reaching to the ceiling with a snapping blaze that helped to add a note of comfort to her otherwise sterile surroundings. Coqui sipped her black coffee, pulled out her phone, and called the office.

"Morning, boss," answered Mateo Daroca, her business partner and best friend since middle school. "How was the sticks?"

"Still here," answered Coqui through a swallow of coffee. Truth be told, she was not his boss. They were equal partners in Jones & Daroca Investigative Services, but he claimed she was smarter than he was. She was by no means smarter, but she was way more disciplined and saw things with a clearer eye. Since his accident, Mateo viewed situations and people more through shades of gray.

"So, tell me about Blythe Rawlins," he said.

Coqui laughed. "Like a true-to-life caricature of a Southern redneck."

"Ouch, that bad, huh?" said Mateo.

"That bad," she repeated. "But I was able to fill in a few details before she passed out."

Mateo tried to cover his fit of laughter, but his voice was too deep. "Sorry," he apologized, with just a hint of the snicker remaining.

Despite herself, Coqui joined in. She told Mateo what she'd learned. "See what you can find out about a family named Watkins – in particular their daughter, Brenda." Coqui had already read the official report by Benjamin Holbrook, the Chief of Police in charge at the time of the investigation. He'd died ten years ago in a boating accident.

"Got it," said Mateo. "When will you be back?"

She sighed. "Hopefully, I'll be wrapped up here in a couple of hours. So, no later than one if I can help it."

"Want to grab lunch when you get here?" he asked.

"Sure." She paused before continuing. "Have you heard from Jenny?"

"Not a word, but I wouldn't worry just yet," said Mateo. "She's twenty-three years old."

"But she has the mind of an eleven-year-old," Coqui shot back.

"Yeah, but I think you don't give her enough credit. She's –"

"I don't want to discuss it right now," said Coqui.

"Fine. Call me when you get close." He hung up.

A dread spread over Coqui. Jenny Davidson was her "adopted" special needs little sister. She lived in Just People, a facility that housed individuals who couldn't live on their own for a variety of reasons. Jenny's apartment was in a community compound with around-the-clock supervision and security. Coqui was part of a volunteer one-on-one mentoring program that helped these adult-children establish a full life for themselves. She and Jenny had been together for almost two years.

Coqui sent up a prayer for Jenny's protection, and then she got up to refill her mug. Settling back into the sofa, she pulled out the notes she had accumulated so far on this case.

Dexter Sterling had been born in Opelika, Florida in 1950, played defensive end on his high school football team, but dropped out his junior year, leaving home when he was seventeen. Over the next few years he collected a half dozen arrests for minor incidents. Like Blythe said, Dexter had been a drifter who never stayed in one place too long.

Coqui studied a picture of him taken from his 1966 yearbook. He was in a group shot and wore his football uniform, towering well above his teammates. He had black hair, a square-cut jaw, and a set of expansive shoulders.

"You still here?" came a voice from behind her.

"Morning, Mrs. Rawlins," answered Coqui without looking up. "You sleep alright?"

"Like a baby," Blythe answered. "Thought you'd be on the road by now."

"We didn't finish our conversation last night."

The old woman shrugged and shuffled her way to the urn. As she poured coffee, she grumbled, "Already told you everythin.'"

"We never talked about the night of the murder." Coqui put away her notes on Dexter, and then removed the legal pad with the notes from her conversation with Blythe.

Blythe sat down, crossed her legs, and sipped the coffee. "I'm sure you've read the report." She, too, wore her clothes from the previous night. The pilled, gray sweater covered a plaid, cotton dress that hung mid-calf. Spider veins marbled her crepey, white legs. Dark, slouchy socks pooled over her worn-out tennis shoes. Coqui winced as Blythe slurped her first taste of coffee. Evidently, her roomie hadn't bothered with a shower this morning, or any other routine personal hygiene for that matter.

"Yes, I've read the report," Coqui confirmed. "Several times, but I want to hear it from you."

Blythe shook her head and arched her eyebrows. "Julie Ann was home from college on Christmas break. She'd been in bed with a stomach flu. That day she'd felt better, so she decided to go out with friends. When she got home, she noticed all the lights were on in the trailer. She went inside, and the livin' room was in an uproar – turned over furniture, broken glass – and she heard shouting from Earlene's bedroom. She knew her mama and Dexter were at it again. Julie Ann went in the bedroom and saw them strugglin' over a gun. She joined in, tryin' to pull Dexter off Earlene. Somewhere in the scuffle, Dexter shoved Julie Ann and she fell down, hittin' the back of her head and blackin' out. When she came to, she was on the floor. Dexter lay in a pool of blood with a bullet hole in his chest. Earlene was holdin' the gun."

"And that's when you came in?" asked Coqui.

The old woman nodded. "That's right. I lived next door . . . heard Julie Ann's scream. I called Chief Holbrook."

"What happened while you waited for Holbrook?"

"I took them in the livin' room and made them sit down; Julie Ann was hysterical. Earlene was as cool as a cucumber. When I asked what happened, Earlene said she couldn't take any more of his abuse." Blythe's chin quivered. "When Holbrook got there, she made a full confession." Coqui thought she saw a tear roll down the old woman's face.

"The investigation and trial took less than two weeks," prompted Coqui.

"Wasn't much to investigate," said Blythe, mustering up her previous resolve. "Miss Brenda hired a good attorney, but Earlene still got a life sentence."

"I'm surprised the attorney didn't go for a plea of self-defense," said Coqui.

"You'd have to ask the lawyer about that," replied Blythe.

Coqui jotted down a note have Mateo check out Earlene's lawyer while he was collecting information on Brenda Watkins. She scanned what she had written down, and then she leveled her eyes at Blythe. "So, let me make sure I've got this straight. Julie Ann came in, saw the trashed living room, went into Earlene's bedroom, and there she saw her mama and Dexter arguing over a gun. She tried to help, fell because

Dexter pushed her, and she hit her head and blacked out. When she came to, her mama was standing over Dexter's body with the gun she shot him with still in her hand."

Without a moment's hesitation, Blythe nodded. "That's it."

Coqui tapped her pen on the notebook, thinking. "Sounds to me like a lot of women had a reason to want Dexter dead," said Coqui.

"True enough," conceded Blythe, her head bobbing up and down. "But only one was standin' over his body with the murder weapon."

Coqui leaned in closer. "And you heard Julie Ann's scream, but *not* the gun shots?" challenged Coqui. "I find that a little hard to believe. I'd think a gunshot would have been much louder."

"I was in the shower with the radio turned up." Blythe raised the mug to her mouth and sipped. "Just like I told Chief Holbrook twenty-five years ago." She dipped her head toward the papers in Coqui's lap. "Says so right there in the report."

Chapter Three

Coqui returned to her room, showered, and then gathered her belongings. Sitting on the side of the bed, she called Jenny. After four rings, she heard the familiar voice asking the caller to leave a message.

"Hi, Jenny, it's me. Please call," Coqui said. Her voice exuded a light tone to cover her heavy heart. "I just want to know you're okay." She paused, and then ventured, "I'm really sorry about yesterday. I'm not trying to keep you from having a life . . . I only meant . . ." She stopped, rubbing a hand across her forehead. "Please, Jenny, just call."

Coqui disconnected and placed the phone in her tote. No need to revisit the reasons why she "butted in," trying to explain the reasons for her concern for Jenny's safety. Jenny knew enough to drive a car and hold down a job at a local day care center. She knew enough of some things to function just like anyone else. When it came to knowing and being aware of situations and people who might be taking advantage of her, Jenny didn't have a clue and most likely never would. It was a skill she was incapable of learning.

Coqui stood and walked back to the office to turn in the room key. As she entered the lobby, she heard a voice call from the buffet.

"The Watkins are the richest people 'round these parts," called Deborah. "Maybe in the state of Georgia."

Coqui turned around and saw the desk clerk straightening the coffee bar, wiping away the half-used sugar packets and spilled coffee.

She began stacking the dirty mugs, placing the used spoons inside the top cup.

"Sorry," Deborah said, turning to face Coqui. Then in a way of explanation, she continued, "I couldn't help overhearing you and Miss Blythe talking about Dexter's murder earlier. Sheri Barker and I were the friends Julie Ann had been out with that night." Deborah hesitated. "Don't know if it'll help, but I can tell you all I remember."

"Sure," said Coqui, her eyes scanning the room. "Where's Mrs. Rawlins?"

"She went to have breakfast at the diner," answered Deborah still cleaning the buffet.

Coqui nodded as she made her way toward Deborah.

Deborah held up a hand. "No, stay where you are; I'll come over there," she said, "that way I can keep an eye on the front door and catch any incoming calls."

"I'd like to hear anything you have to say," encouraged Coqui.

"The Watkins had everything," Deborah said as she moved in the direction of the reception desk. Her face became serious. "Miss Brenda was their only child and inherited everything."

"Where did the Watkins get all their money?" asked Coqui.

"They had a horse ranch passed down through the family, but the real money came from their properties," said Deborah. "After the Depression, Old Man Watkins," Deborah paused, and she explained the relationships. "Old Man Watkins was Nathaniel Watkins – Miss Brenda's grandfather and Junior Watkins was her dad."

Coqui nodded her understanding.

"So, after the Depression, Old Man Watkins bought up as much land as fast as he could throughout South Georgia and then just sat on it."

"Who eventually bought it?"

"The family sold a good bit when I-75 was being built in the 60's and 70's. Then later Junior sold what lined the interstate to developers who were making strip and outlet malls along there," answered Deborah.

"And Brenda got everything?"

"Kit and caboodle," said Deborah. "Her father Junior was an only child and so was she. She grew up on that ranch. Her parents were strict, but taught her all about riding, shooting, and breeding racehorses. Got a lot of money in stud fees and won a few races. After his stroke, though, he sold most of the stock."

Coqui wrote as Deborah talked about Brenda's life, her teaching degree from Georgia Southern, and then her teaching career at Hampton High School.

When Deborah stopped, Coqui asked, "And Brenda just helped Earlene and Julie Ann out of the goodness of her heart?"

"She was like that." Deborah nodded. "When Earlene got out of the hospital, she would get these headaches . . . so bad she'd have to take to bed. And she was limited as to what she could do while she was healing from the two broken arms. She couldn't take care of Julie Ann, much less hold down a steady job."

"When was this again?" interrupted Coqui.

Deborah pursed her lips and thought for a moment. "I think it was 1988."

"And Brenda Watkins supported them?" asked Coqui.

"Totally. Made sure Julie Ann went to the best schools and wore the finest clothes. She sent in a housekeeper to take care of the cleaning and cooking." Deborah sighed and then smiled. "Miss Brenda helped lots of people around Hampton, but everyone knew Julie Ann was her pick."

"Where are the Watkins now?" asked Coqui.

"All dead except Miss Brenda. She's down at Knollwood Village, the former Watkins estate." Deborah frowned. "But you won't learn much from her." She tapped her temple with a finger. "Dementia."

"Did Brenda Watkins ever visit Earlene in prison?"

"As much as they'd let her, but then her mind got too bad," answered Deborah. "So, Julie Ann kept her eye on her mama, *and* she kept an eye on Miss Brenda." Her eyes softened. "Goes every Saturday." She sighed. "Although I don't think Miss Brenda recognizes her most of the time."

Coqui looked at Deborah. "What's the story with Mrs. Rawlins? Said she was the one who heard Julie Ann's scream. But she *didn't* hear the gun shots."

"That was her story then and that's her story now. There's no one to dispute it. Dexter's dead. Earlene's dead. Chief Holbrook's dead. And Miss Brenda's loony." Deborah tilted her head to one side. "How do you know Julie Ann?"

"I volunteer in a prison ministry project through my church. Met her there several years ago when she was visiting her mama."

"A prison ministry?" Deborah pursed her lips. "Doing what?"

"A small group of us lead a weekly Bible study," replied Coqui.

"And that's where you met Julie Ann?"

Coqui nodded. "Her mama was part of the group. Sometimes Julie Ann would join us."

"But Julie Ann's just now doing something?" asked Deborah.

"Earlene always made her promise not to interfere," explained Coqui. "When she died last week, Julie Ann came to my office. She wants to clear her mama's name."

"And clear her own mind as well."

"I suppose," echoed Coqui.

"Do you remember anything from that night? Anything that might have seemed unusual about Julie Ann or Earlene?"

Deborah shook her head. "No, sorry. Just a regular movie night for three girls home from college. I never even saw her mama. We picked Julie Ann up outside the trailer and then dropped her off a few hours later." Pain filled her eyes. "I didn't even hear about it until the next morning." Another shake of the head. "Not like it is now where everything spreads like wildfire on social media."

Coqui pulled out her card and placed it on the counter. "If you think of anything you think might help, call me."

"I can tell you the name of the other girl who was out with us that night – Sheri Barker, but she moved away about a year later. Never kept in touch." She glanced down at the card. "You're a PI?" She smiled. "The real deal, huh?"

Coqui smiled. "The real deal."

Deborah thumped the card with her finger. "I'll call if I think of something."

"I appreciate it," said Coqui.

Coqui turned and went out the sliding glass doors into the parking lot, heading toward her car, then crawled in and started the engine. Out of the corner of her eye she saw a bent-over figure crunching through the gravel parking lot from the diner toward Cooter's. Apparently, Blythe thought she had sobered up enough to drive her own car back home. Coqui eased her car up beside the old woman and then rolled down the window.

"Want a lift to Cooter's?" asked Coqui. Cooter's was across the street, with a busy highway in between.

Blythe looked up into a low-hung, gray cloud sky. She pursed her lips and shook her head no. "I think I'd rather walk." She reached in her cardigan sweater's pocket and pulled out a cigarette, placing it between her lips. "Headin' home?" she asked.

"For now," answered Coqui. "I'll be visiting Knollwood Village tomorrow."

"You're not goin' to learn anythin' from Miss Brenda. She wasn't there that night. As much as she helped Julie Ann and her mama, she never set foot in their trailer." She slid a lighter from her dress's pocket. "I *was* there, not Miss Brenda, *and* I've told you everythin'." She flipped opened the lighter, placing the flame at the tip of the cigarette. She inhaled deeply and held her breath, finally exhaling. "Nothin' like that first drag of the day." She clicked the lighter closed and returned it to her pocket.

"I wouldn't know," said Coqui. "Never smoked."

"There's a lot you don't know, missy," smirked Blythe. "Sometimes it's best to let sleepin' dogs lie." She turned to leave but stopped and called over her shoulder. "By the way, thanks for my sleepin' arrangements last night. But don't think that means I owe you anythin.'"

"You don't owe me a thing, Mrs. Rawlins, but you might owe something to Julie Ann since you and her mama were like this." Coqui held up two fingers and wiggled them side-by-side.

Chapter Four

Coqui got on I-75 and headed north to Decatur, where she lived and where she and Mateo maintained their offices. She adjusted the volume on the classical radio station to low, settling in for her return drive home. Hopefully, she'd catch that window of "no traffic," the space between morning and evening rush hours. In Atlanta, one never knew. Most times that window seemed to open and close with no rhyme or reason.

She thought about lives like Earlene's and Julie Ann's. The same question always popped up. *Why is it that misfortune seems to follow some people around with few breaks in between?* Through seemingly no fault of their own, some people just seem to get dealt crappy lives. As a Christian, that was perhaps the most difficult question to answer or to defend, especially to herself. She whispered John 16:33 aloud.

"I have told you these things, so that in me you may have peace. In this world, you will have trouble. But take heart! I have overcome the world."

But that didn't seem to satisfy most people. Often, it didn't satisfy Coqui either. She wanted things to fall into good and bad, and right and wrong. She wanted to see people get what they deserved. Too many good people drew the shortest straws while bad people never got caught or had to pay the consequences. When she'd decided to open Investigative Services, her goal was to bring justice where it was needed.

She been raised by the Golden Rule and turn the other cheek Bible verses. It was what she hung onto, and what she believed.

Her mind wandered to her own childhood. She'd had the perfect life in a loving, nurturing, and solidly middle-class family. Her mama was a nurse, and her dad a history teacher and wrestling coach at Decatur High School.

Then her junior year at Georgia State University, lightning struck the tree outside her parents' bedroom. The tree crashed on their roof, killing both while they slept. The house burned to the ground, with nothing remaining. Coqui had escaped uninjured. For years, she'd tried to make sense of the situation, but in the end, she supposed it was just "one of those things." End of story. No one to blame. Life goes on . . . but in a much, much different direction.

She'd graduated from college and banked the monies she'd collected from her parents' life insurance policy and the sale of the lot on which the house had burned down. She moved into a tiny apartment, and using her degree in sociology, she volunteered in several of her church's local outreach ministries. It was through the Special Needs ministry that she met Bill Davidson.

Bill was in his early fifties, divorced, and a personal injury attorney. He was also Jenny's father. Seven years ago, Bill hit the "big one" in a case against a large pharmaceutical company and never needed to work again. He bought a rundown, abandoned mansion sitting on an even more rundown property on Ponce de Leon Avenue. He cleared the land and built Just People, an enclave of 20 units for Special Needs adults. He now lived upstairs in the renovated mansion. The bottom floor was the reception area and business offices for Just People. He wanted to live out the rest of his life raising awareness for these unique individuals.

Coqui assisted him with whatever he needed. In exchange, Bill gave her the two-bedroom space in what had been the Carriage House on the original estate and let her and Mateo have their Investigative

Service offices on the main floor of the mansion rent free. It was during this period she'd become Jenny's mentor, a woman with a dynamite body and looks paired with a perpetually adolescent immaturity.

Jenny had met a man at the day care center, a father of one of the children. He'd taken Jenny out, explaining that he was divorced. After a little probing, Coqui discovered he was still married. Thus, yesterday's explosion. Instead of blaming the adulterous husband, Jenny had blamed Coqui for trying to run her life.

Coqui exited I-285 to I-20, heading west. Her phone rang: Caller ID – Mateo.

Coqui answered. "What's up?"

"You close?" he asked.

"Another 25 minutes, maybe."

"Why don't I meet you at Sweet Melissa's. I made an appointment for Augustus at the vet's," Mateo explained. "He's been scratching his left ear. Dr. Lynn said she could take a look at him now if I could bring him over."

"Sure, see you there when you're finished."

Augustus was Mateo's Labrador Retriever. He was also his canine assistant. Mateo received his law degree from the University of Georgia but had chosen to work toward a career as a detective with the Atlanta Police Department. Unfortunately, after several years on the force, a bullet shattered not only his dream, but his spine as well.

Augustus was barrel-chested and 150 pounds of pure muscle. He went everywhere that Mateo went except when his owner needed to be out of town. On those occasions, Augustus stayed with Coqui.

Coqui drove around Decatur Square. Today was her lucky day: she found an empty parking space directly in front of Sweet Melissa's. She pulled in, fed the meter, and walked into the restaurant.

Sweet Melissa's opened in 1989 and served breakfast and lunch daily. On Sundays, there was live music and a crowd of waiting patrons. Coqui found a table and settled in.

"Hi, Coqui," said Denise. "Just you today?"

Coqui shook her head no. "Mateo will be joining me."

While Denise set down their menus, Coqui ordered a sparkling water. "Bring Mateo a sweet tea," she said.

Denise smiled. "And extra lemon."

As Coqui scanned the menu, her stomach rumbled. Realizing she'd missed breakfast, she settled on two tilapia tacos and a side of fries. It dawned on her that she'd skipped her morning run as well. She'd have to work it in tonight, and then she changed her mind from the fries to a side salad.

Coqui looked up and saw Mateo rolling up to the table. His cologne drifted her way, and he smiled. As he positioned his wheelchair closer to the table, Augustus settled in beside him.

"Wait long?" asked Mateo.

Coqui shook her head no. "Just got here."

Denise brought their drinks and then took their orders.

Coqui patted Augustus's beefy side. "Well, what's the verdict?" she asked, shifting her attention to Mateo.

"Ear infection," he replied.

Coqui winced. "That means I have to give him drops next week while you're in D.C."

Mateo held up two hands and shrugged. "Sorry."

Augustus's ears flattened, and he peered up through pitiful eyes.

Mateo laughed. "I sent you everything I found out on the Watkins, particularly Brenda." He leaned back as Denise set their food before him. He looked up and smiled. "Thanks."

"I thought you were laying off the burgers," said Coqui as she studied his mushroom, Swiss cheese, and bacon concoction. "And onion rings, too?"

"Livy's in Costa Rica for the month," he said, plucking a fried ringlet from his plate and then crunching it into his mouth.

"Oh, yeah." Livy was Mateo's girlfriend. Then she asked, "So, is this Brenda the saint they all claim?"

"Apparently," said Mateo. "What did you learn from Mrs. Rawlins?"

"Nothing. She repeats the same thing that is in the police report as if it were a script," said Coqui. "And that's what bothers me. It's too pat."

"Maybe because that's what happened," said Mateo.

"Maybe."

"Is there anyone else who could have done it?" asked Mateo. "A motive?"

"I thought maybe the woman Dexter sent to the Emergency Room years before he hooked up with Earlene the first time."

"Shirley Finney," said Mateo.

"That's her name?" asked Coqui.

He nodded. "And she waits all those years, returns, shoots Dexter, puts the gun in Earlene's hand, and flees the scene never to be heard from again?" Pursing his lips, he continued, "I don't buy it." Mateo tapped his index finger on the table. "But I put what I found on her along with the rest of the information I sent you."

Coqui didn't say anything, raking her fork through the salad and removing all the red onions, shoving them to the edges of her bowl.

"And you don't buy it either," said Mateo.

She glared across the table, taking in Mateo's dark brown eyes. "What am I supposed to do?" asked Coqui, laying down her fork. "I promised Julie Ann I'd clear her mama's name."

"Not so." Mateo wiped his mouth with the napkin. Placing both his elbows on the table, he leaned in. "You promised to look into the old files, talk to people, and see if anything new has come to light. Maybe Earlene is the killer."

"That's what everyone says," objected Coqui.

"Maybe because that's the truth," Mateo shot back. His tone softened. "Do what you promised – *check out* the old files and people. Then report back to Julie Ann what you find."

Coqui knew he was right, she just hated to admit it. She shoved the last bite of her taco into her mouth, and then turned up the remainder of her sparkling water. "I have a couple other names for you to check out."

Mateo nodded. "On another note," he began. "I've tailed Raleigh Studebaker for the last week."

"Yeah, Jenny's divorced suitor," said Coqui sarcastically, her fingers crooked around the word "divorced."

"He's definitely not divorced, or separated," said Mateo, pulling out his phone. He opened his pictures folder and slid the phone to Coqui.

Coqui looked at photo after photo of Raleigh, his two toddlers, and his very pregnant wife. One was of him and his wife out to dinner at an intimate and expensive restaurant. A video captured them walking in the parking lot with their arms entwined, hips bumping, and lips locked as they made their way to their minivan.

"Jerk," said Coqui, returning the phone to Mateo.

Chapter Five

Coqui returned to her office around 4:00 and called Knollwood Village to make an appointment to meet with Brenda Watkins the next day at eleven. The receptionist, Gretchen Springfield, said she couldn't promise what state Miss Brenda's mind would be in, but that by coming later in the morning, Coqui should get that brief window of opportunity where the residents were the most lucid and agreeable.

Checking that off her list, Coqui settled in at her desk, ready to organize her notes and impressions from her talk with Blythe Rawlins. She reviewed the files on Dexter Sterling, Police Chief Holbrook's report, and the transcripts from the trial. She also read the information on the Watkins. Mateo had done his usual thorough job, never leaving a stone unturned or a nook not searched. She placed her elbows on the desk and stared out into nothing in particular. She felt like she didn't know any more than she had before she'd walked into the doors of Cooter's last night, and the thought didn't sit well with her.

Like she'd told Mateo, everything seemed to be so cut and dried, all the pieces fitting together way too conveniently. True, Dexter Sterling had been bad news from the get-go, and no one shed a tear over his death. But Earlene? Surely, the attorney should have gone for a plea of self-defense.

Coqui paused and thought about another question that had been bothering her. Why had Dexter shown up after six years? He'd left in 1975 after putting Shirley Finney in the hospital and returned in 1988 when the children of a woman he'd been living with in North Carolina found out he'd been draining their mom's retirement. He'd returned to Hampton and shacked up with Earlene. Yet again, he'd been forced to flee, this time the battered woman was Julie Ann's mom. Coqui needed to find out what brought Dexter back in 1994. After all, he'd left with the possibility of battery charges hanging over him.

Coqui considered this for a few minutes, running several scenarios through her mind. Maybe he wasn't returning to Hampton as she'd originally thought; perhaps he was running from some other trouble. After all, that seemed to be the man's pattern. She drummed her fingers on her desk and then rolled back in her chair, opening a side drawer and taking out a stack of note cards. She removed the top one and wrote: Murder Suspects.

Earlene Thornton – Okay, like it or not, she did confess to the murder. She had motive and opportunity, and her daughter was an eyewitness after the fact to her standing over the body holding the gun in her hand.

Shirley Finney – the woman Dexter sent to the ER in 1975 – While it was a possibility and she had a good motive for killing her attacker, Coqui didn't really think this woman was a strong possibility. If she'd wanted to seek revenge, why wait 19 years? Why go over to Earlene's trailer that night where there would be a witness? And, why would Earlene take the fall for her?

Which brought Coqui to the next possibility.

Julie Ann – As much as she didn't like the idea of suspecting that her client might be the murderer, Julie Ann could have been the one to shoot Dexter during the struggle, black out, and then come to and not remember anything except seeing her mother over the body. Giving Earlene a very good reason to confess so that there wouldn't be an investigation.

Blythe – Just because Coqui didn't like the woman, didn't mean she was the murderer. But she'd admitted during their conversation that she and Earlene both had had crushes on him back in high school. Jealousy? Coqui shuddered at the thought of that old crone ever having had a love life.

Unknown Assailant – If Dexter had been running away from trouble in 1994, perhaps he'd angered someone enough to follow him to Georgia and kill him. But again, it made no sense for Earlene to take the blame.

Coqui sighed and reread the reports Mateo had given her. While she was reading the police file, she noticed something that she'd overlooked before. The only prints on the murder weapon were Earlene's. If there'd been a struggle, then Dexter's should have been on there as well. Had the gun been wiped clean and Earlene's prints planted on the handle? If Julie Ann had shot Dexter that would make sense as to why other prints might have been removed.

Coqui straightened the note cards in front of her and closed her eyes. She really didn't like the direction her investigation was leading her. Like it or not, she needed to have a long talk with Julie Ann to see exactly what she remembered.

The sun was dipping lower toward the trees outside her office. If she was going to get in her run, she'd need to leave now. Coqui straightened her desk and locked the door behind her as she left. Having her office only fifty yards from where she lived had really worked out well. When she agreed to the arrangement three years ago, she wasn't sure if she'd like living and working so close to her landlord and boss. Bill Davidson had turned out to be the best in both of those worlds, as well as becoming a great friend and father figure.

Coqui crunched across the gravel parking lot toward the carriage house. There was a space underneath the residence where carriages had been taken, but it now served her well as a carport. She mounted the stairs and unlocked the front door. A chill had settled over the place in her absence, so she adjusted the heat as she passed by the thermostat. Changing into her leggings and a long-sleeved t-shirt, she bent over, laced her running shoes, and stood, grabbing her phone as she went out the door.

The temperatures had dropped since the sun set. Coqui rubbed her hands together briskly and puffed a couple of hot breaths into her palms to generate heat into her fingers. She began at a slow pace to warm up her leg muscles and work out the stiffness in her lower back and shoulders from too much sitting in the last twenty-four hours. Fall was her favorite time of the year, especially for running – a bit of a nip on the skin that grew into a warm fire burning her from the inside out.

Coqui ran down the sidewalk on Ponce de Leon Avenue, the street their property faced. Traffic poked along with Sunday cruisers inching their way home. The street ran through several small burbs that led into the city of Atlanta. She made her way over to Decatur Square, passing the historic courthouse and smelling the aromas drifting from the kitchens of the variety of restaurants that lined her route. She cut over to Church Street, passed the Presbyterian Church, and took a left onto Trinity, passing Twain's and a midrise apartment building. Looking both ways, she crossed the railroad tracks to Agnes Scott College.

Agnes Scott was founded in 1889 and had remained a women's private liberal arts college. Coqui loved the feel of running by the school with its tree-lined streets and old-world campus. She'd taken enough literature and writing classes to earn a second major in English. If she ever decided on a career change, she'd want to be a professor in a small, rural college.

Coqui could feel the sweat beading on her forehead and the burn in her lungs and hamstrings as she pumped her legs harder. This was her favorite route of all her runs. Her mind worked to release the stresses of the day and wrap itself around the Bon Jovi song playing through her earbuds. By the time she made the turn to double back homeward, the wind had picked up and blew into her face, the music setting a rhythm for her feet and melting the day's frustrations. While she'd never experienced that runner's high that so many speak of, she did reach a place where her mind could sand away the sharp, jagged thoughts that prickled her calm.

Fifteen minutes later, her watch vibrated, indicating the end of her run. She slowed to a trot, and then to a walk. She reached the intersection of Ponce de Leon and Church once more. She pushed the pedestrian walk button for the light to turn green. While she waited, she stretched her legs, studying the crowd at Leon's, a popular local restaurant. Diners packed the outside area while they listened for their names to be called. Most chatted in small groups, with drinks in their hands. Four patrons whiled away their wait with a game of bocce ball. On one of the benches sat a couple in a long embrace, the man stroking and kissing the woman's face and neck.

Coqui's stomach lurched. The lovey-dovey couple was Jenny and Raleigh. Her first instinct was to dart through the traffic and expose the low life for what he was and force him to confess his lies. She paused, said a prayer, and let her yoga training bring her breathing and heart rate down. Going over there with her feelings flaming and still having Jenny angry with her could cause more harm to their relationship and more good to hers and Raleigh's. She watched them until Jenny and Raleigh went inside when their table was ready. She might not join them, but she wasn't going to leave them unwatched.

Coqui snagged an outside table at the restaurant on the opposite corner from Leon's, and then ordered a salad and a glass of wine. She finished her salad and looked at her phone. They'd only been inside half an hour.

The server interrupted her guard. "Will there be anything else?" he asked.

"Another glass of wine, please," she said, her cheeks reddening at being caught spying.

Coqui remained at her table, nursing the second glass of wine. After an hour, Jenny and Raleigh emerged and walked arm-in-arm to the public parking lot. Scenes of Deja-vu returned as she thought of the video Mateo had shown her at lunch only the caressing arm had been attached to his wife's hip.

Coqui tossed money on the table and then lagged behind them from across the street at a safe distance. She watched as Raleigh escorted Jenny to her car. Another long kiss before he gently closed the car door and left, giving her a little finger wave as he turned. Once Jenny started her car and pulled away, Coqui had no choice but to resume her trek homeward.

When she arrived at the Just People complex, Coqui circled to the back building where Jenny's apartment was located. She breathed a sigh of relief when she saw Jenny's car in its usual space.

Coqui dialed Mateo.

"You need to pay Raleigh a visit and give him an incentive to move on . . . now."

Chapter Six

The following morning, Coqui got up and prepared for her return trip to Hampton and her visit with Brenda Watkins. She didn't know what she expected to learn. According to those who'd known Brenda Watkins, the mind that had once been razor-sharp now struggled to hold a thought. When she saw the sign for Hampton, Coqui exited and headed for Knollwood Village.

Knollwood Village was nestled amid a thicket of pine trees with gardens and gazebos scattered around the property. A large lake spread to one side and a barn with a couple of horses tussling playfully in a fenced-in area occupied the opposite side. The home itself was a white brick, colonial-style structure. The landscape was well manicured and the physical facility pristine.

As Coqui eased from her car, a chilly breeze stroked her cheeks, bringing with it a smattering of tiny raindrops. She pulled up the hood of her jacket and slung her bag over her shoulder, crunching her way across the parking lot toward a set of stairs leading to an expansive front porch. Rocking chairs lined up in a row like soldiers appearing for roll call, most filled by residents wearing sweat suits and tennis shoes. Some carried on conversations; most, however, simply stared into space. A voice broke Coqui's reverie.

"May I help you?" a woman in a pale blue uniform asked. She tilted her head to one side.

Coqui felt as if she'd been caught spying. Placing both hands to her chest, she approached the woman, and smiled. "I'm sorry. I should have come inside first." She extended a business card toward the woman, and Coqui read the plastic name badge pinned to her shirt: Gretchen.

"Ah, Ms. Springfield. I'm Coqui Jones." Coqui held out her hand and continued, "We spoke on the phone yesterday afternoon."

Gretchen Springfield nodded and smiled. "You're here to see Miss Brenda." Tears filled her eyes, and then she added, "The sweetest and most generous woman God ever placed on His green earth."

"I heard how she cared for Julie Ann and her mother," said Coqui.

"And about half the folks in Hampton." She spread her arms wide. "This property is her former home. People pay only what they can afford. When my daddy lost his job in the eighties, she gave him work. He still stays on as head caretaker of Knollwood Village, and I manage it. Miss Brenda also took care of my mama throughout the cancer that eventually took her life, and she sent me and my two brothers to college."

"Is it going to be possible for me to see her?" asked Coqui.

The woman nodded and motioned for Coqui to follow her through the double doors leading into the house.

The entry was a large foyer that soared all the way to the third floor with a massive crystal chandelier suspended from a domed ceiling. The inside was as spotless as the outside, but the decorating gave the facility a warm, inviting feel. A spiral staircase ascended to the second and third floors. Off from the foyer was a main room with a large, flat screen television, a couple of sofas, and several reclining chairs.

To the other side of the foyer was the dining room. The mahogany table was set for twelve, complete with a white linen cloth and fresh bright yellow mums in the center. From the aroma drifting to her nose, Coqui assumed the kitchen was beyond that room.

She breathed in deeply and smiled.

"That's Miss Betsy's homemade vegetable soup," said Gretchen. "Today we're serving it with cornbread and apple pie with vanilla bean ice cream."

"It smells wonderful," Coqui swooned, trying to keep from drooling.

"You're welcome to join us after you talk with Miss Brenda," invited Ms. Springfield. "This way," she motioned with a crooked finger as she walked down a hallway to the back of the house.

Outside the kitchen toward the rear entrance hung a long row of coat hooks attached to a two-by-four wooden board nailed to the wall. Underneath the jackets, scarves, and gloves stood an assortment of rain boots and umbrellas.

Ms. Springfield pointed to the coat area. "You can put your things here."

"Thanks," said Coqui, removing her jacket and draping it over a hook.

Gretchen nodded and pressed a button; an elevator door opened.

"Miss Brenda took the room she had as a girl. After Miss Earlene's trial, she began the project to convert the house into a home for the infirm." She looked into Coqui's eyes. "This isn't an old folks' home. Anyone who requires fulltime attention qualifies."

Coqui nodded.

"Miss Brenda's room is the only resident room on the top floor, except for my daddy's; he has a room up here, too. The rest of the rooms are used for storage and office space," she added.

The door to Brenda Watkins's room stood ajar. "Miss Brenda?" Gretchen called. And then she rapped gently. "You've got a visitor." She opened the door the rest of the way.

In a chair, next to a set of French doors, sat Brenda Watkins. She turned her head and smiled.

Even hunkered over in her wheelchair, you could see that Brenda Watkins had been a statuesque woman in her prime, not fat, just large.

She had her hands folded in her lap, and on her feet, she wore white Velcro tennis shoes. The steel gray hair was scraped into a bun at the nape of her neck, and her face revealed nothing as to what was in store for Coqui's visit.

"May we come in?" asked Ms. Springfield.

The old woman nodded. A musky scent coming from a candle burning on the coffee table sent out an aroma that almost covered the disinfectant's smell.

"Miss Brenda, this is Coqui Jones. She's a friend of Julie Ann's."

Coqui thought she saw a flash of recognition at the mention of Julie Ann's name.

"Julie Ann comes every Saturday to see Miss Brenda," said Ms. Springfield more for the old woman's benefit than Coqui's.

Poor Julie Ann thought Coqui. If she'd visited her mother a couple of times a week and Brenda Watkins once a week, no wonder she'd never built a life of her own. Coqui's heart squeezed. Since her parents' deaths ten years ago, she'd not built a life either.

Ms. Springfield pointed to a chair. "Please, sit." Coqui sat down and faced Brenda Watkins. "This lady has some questions for you."

Coqui shifted in the chair, not exactly sure how to begin. "Ms. Watkins—"

She held up a wrinkled hand, fingers crooked and joints swollen. A small smile tugged at the corners of her lips. "My mind comes and goes . . . better some days than others. Ask what you want . . . quickly . . . you seem to have gotten me at a good time."

"Julie Ann thinks her mama didn't kill Dexter Sterling. She thinks someone else did and has asked me to look into it," Coqui explained.

"Give the child back her money. Earlene's gone . . . the time's been served . . . it's over." Her voice was firm and flat, her tone final.

Coqui paused, waiting for another objection. Receiving none, she ventured, "I've spoken to Blythe Rawlins."

Ms. Watkins chuckled, her shoulders shaking ever so slightly. "Her memory's worse than mine."

"Her story's the backbone for the official report," said Coqui.

"Let it go," she warned, her meaning crystal clear.

Coqui sighed. "All Julie Ann remembers is entering a ravaged living room and walking in on her mama and Dexter Sterling arguing over the gun. She blacked out and awoke to Dexter dead and Earlene holding a gun. Then, Blythe Rawlins appeared, telephoned Chief Holbrook, and took them into the living room. Julie Ann's mind is pretty much a blank otherwise."

Ms. Watkins shook her head. "I have nothing that can make Julie Ann feel better." A tear rolled down her cheek. "And I've told her that a hundred times." Her voice became agitated as she wrung her hands. "Gretchen, please take me to my bed."

"I'm sorry," apologized Ms. Springfield. "I'm afraid Miss Brenda's upset."

Coqui nodded.

"No, wait," called Ms. Watkins, changing her direction as she wheeled across the room. She went to a framed picture on her dresser. The photograph was of a much younger Brenda Watkins, Earlene, and Julie Ann, all three wearing blue and green tartan plaid wool scarves. Brenda Watkins and Julie Ann were so much larger, Earlene looked like a small child tucked between them.

"That picture was taken about a week before Dexter's murder." Her lips froze into a thin flat line as she handed the picture to Coqui. "I bought these scarves for us . . . a Christmas present a couple of weeks before . . ." She took the picture from Coqui's hand and returned it to the dresser.

"It was the last time I saw Julie Ann until she moved in with me after Chief Holbrook arrested Earlene." She sighed. "She never went back to the trailer. Couldn't bear the thought of it."

"What happened to the trailer," asked Coqui. "All their things?"

"After the crime scene people took what they needed, and after the trial was over, I sent in a cleaning company. Julie Ann didn't want to go through the personal belongings." Ms. Watkins shrugged. "Said just sell everything. I couldn't do it. It was all the child had. But I didn't want to go through everything either. I'd never been there, saw no need to start then. So, I rented a storage unit, hired a moving company, and had them take everything there."

"Do you still have the storage area?" asked Coqui.

She nodded. "I gave Julie Ann the key then sold the trailer and gave her the money."

She began wringing her hands faster, tears returning in the corners of her eyes.

Ms. Springfield said, "I think you should rest now, Miss Brenda." She looked at Coqui over the old woman's head.

Coqui walked closer and placed a hand on Ms. Watkins's shoulder. "Thank you."

Coqui went down the back stairway to retrieve her jacket from the coat rack. As she reached for it, she recognized the blue and green tartan scarf she seen in the photograph.

Chapter Seven

Once back in her office, Coqui found a set of papers on Shirley Finney, the woman Dexter had beaten up. Before she read the information, however, she wanted to put in a call to Julie Ann.

Coqui entered the numbers into her phone.

"National Financial Services. How may I direct your call?" the receptionist asked.

"Julie Ann Thornton, please," replied Coqui.

Coqui listened to an instrumental rendition of "Yesterday" as she held on the line. She didn't have to wait long.

"Good afternoon. Julie Ann Thornton," a voice answered.

"Julie Ann, this is Coqui."

Julie Ann's tone changed from professional to more familiar as she asked, "Have you found out anything new?'

"I've followed all the original information you gave me," she said hesitantly, "but I need to ask you some questions to fill in gaps I've come across."

"Sure," agreed Julie Ann. "I'll tell you anything I can remember."

"Do you still have the key to the storage unit Brenda Watkins rents to store the things from your mama's trailer?"

"Yes."

"Would you mind giving it to me so that I can go down and look through what's there?" asked Coqui.

"Of course, if you think it'll help."

"You've never looked at any of those things?" asked Coqui.

"No," said Julie Ann. "It's just too painful to see . . ." She was stopped by a catch in her voice. The line remained awkwardly silent. Then she continued, "To see Mama's things."

"Didn't she ever ask about any of her stuff?" asked Coqui.

"No, I guess it was painful for her, too." Julie Ann sighed. "What's the use in it?"

Coqui let it go. "When can we meet?"

"I'm slammed this afternoon and I'm meeting with a couple of potential clients for dinner tonight. How about I run by your office around nine in the morning?"

"See you then," said Coqui.

Coqui entered Julie Ann's name into her calendar and then turned her attention to Shirley Finney's file, the woman Dexter had hospitalized in the summer of 1975.

Shirley Finney was born in 1953 in Hampton, Georgia to an unwed fifteen-year-old girl. The father's name was entered as "Unknown." Shirley bounced around from foster home to foster home until she was sixteen. On her sixteenth birthday, she quit school and set out on her own. According to the comments from the series of foster parents, Shirley was never a problem, always doing what she was told.

There were no juvenile offenses, and school reports assessed her as a well-behaved, but poor student. Until she hooked up with Dexter Sterling, there were no other accounts about anything she did. Then in 1975, there was the hospital incident. A neighbor had called in a possible domestic violence situation. When the police and paramedics arrived, Shirley was alone – Dexter Sterling was nowhere in sight.

Shirley refused to file a complaint and adamantly denied any sort of abuse. She'd insisted she'd fallen off a chair trying to reach something on a high shelf in the kitchen. According to the hospital's release form, Shirley was treated for a broken nose, severe bruising, and she'd received stitches for three deep cuts. While she refused to file charges or give out a name, people felt it was clearly Dexter Sterling's handiwork. Without charges, however, the then Chief of Police Holbrook could do nothing.

After that there was very little about her. She'd worked as a checkout cashier for a national grocery store chain, and never left Hampton. Mateo had included an address and a phone number. Coqui finished reading the information on Dexter Sterling. She sat up straight and rubbed the back of her neck, her eyes scanning the clock for the time. She should probably get a move on.

Coqui called Shirley Finney, but only reached her voicemail. She left her name, phone number, and the reason for her call. Next, she returned to the file on Dexter Sterling. He had a lengthy record of counts of abuse against women, but in the end the women had dropped all charges.

Coqui's phone rang: Mateo.

"What's up" she asked.

"Want to meet at Ricco's Tapas tonight?" he asked.

"Sure," she answered. "Did you talk to Raleigh?"

"Yep. I'll fill you in tonight."

Coqui went home to freshen up before heading out to Ricco's. She slipped off her heels as she walked to her bedroom. She pulled on jeans and a black turtleneck sweater, and then she walked out onto her balcony to relax before joining Mateo. Slumping down into a chair, she studied her surroundings. The Just People complex spread out before her with a small lake and park in the center, with the mansion's barn and other buildings forming a semi-circle.

When Bill Davidson had designed his project, he wanted to create a healthy, safe, and normal-as-possible life for special needs adults. The original mansion and its buildings faced the busy Ponce de Leon Avenue and the lake was behind the compound.

He'd built the five separate dorms in town house style. Each unit housed four studio apartments for individual residents and a larger unit for the chaperone couples that lived on the bottom floor. He had carefully selected his caregivers. He had included housekeepers, maintenance, counselors, life coaches, ministers, cooks, and law enforcement people to live on the property twenty-four/seven. All workers received their apartments and food free, along with a generous salary.

Coqui thought about Brenda Watkins and how she had used her money to help the infirm. It was people like Bill and Brenda who gave hope and strength for a better world. Those were the people Coqui wanted to align herself with. These individuals might not find their names or deeds appearing in magazines, social media, or the television and cable networks, but they were truly "the beautiful people" not only in God's world, but the human world as well.

Her phone rang. She didn't recognize the number.

"Coqui Jones," she answered.

"Ah . . . er, this is Shirley Finney."

"Yes," said Coqui, straightening in her chair. "Thank you for returning my call."

"I don't know what I can do," Shirley said. Her voice was slow and soft, laced with a deep Southern drawl. Her tone was cautious, implying that she felt like she might be in trouble somehow, sounding like someone who apologized for everything and anything that went wrong.

Coqui explained in more detail what she needed and assured her that any information she gave would only be used to help try and clear Earlene Thornton of the Dexter Sterling's murder.

"Would it be possible to meet with you tomorrow?" asked Coqui.

"What time?"

Coqui thought about her meeting with Julie Ann. "After one?"

"I don't have to be in to work until four, so yeah, one works," said Shirley.

Coqui thanked her and clicked off the phone. Looking at the time, she realized she was late for meeting Mateo. She hurriedly put on her boots and headed out the door.

Chapter Eight

E ven running late, Coqui arrived at Ricco's before Mateo. She found an empty table near the back of the restaurant and signaled Jason, their regular server. Ricco's was a newer place in the area, but it had caught on well. They offered small plates, mostly with a Caribbean flavor and maintained a fine wine selection.

Jason set the usual glass of white wine before Coqui.

She looked up and smiled. "Thanks." Raising the glass to her lips, she sipped as she savored that first taste.

Her mind traveled to thoughts of her meeting with Julie Ann the following morning. She didn't think opening with the line, "I've put you on my list of murder suspects" was a great lead-in. What Coqui really needed was to focus on was the time Julie Ann blacked out and why she'd been knocked unconscious in the first placed. She thought it was a result of the struggle between her mama and Dexter, but she should see if there was more to the story.

So far, all she knew was that Julie Ann had gotten out of the car with her friends, entered the trailer, and saw that the living room was in disarray. She had heard shouting from Earlene and Dexter and went into the bedroom where she walked in on them struggling with a gun.

Coqui's mind did a freeze-frame. Where had the gun come from in the first place? Who did it belong to? Dexter? Had he brought the gun with him? Did he threaten Earlene? Or was it the other way around?

Had he threatened Earlene and she herself had a gun and pulled it out to use on him?

She toyed with the stem of her wine glass as her mind followed those thoughts. If Dexter had only been coming over to find a place to stay, why the need for a gun in the first place? Another scenario – perhaps he'd just shown up and Earlene had run into her bedroom to get a gun for protection or in an effort to scare him away.

She thought back to the police report. She didn't remember anything specific about the gun only that it had been the murder weapon and it had Earlene's fingerprints on it.

She needed to find the answers to two vital questions. Where did the gun come from? Why had Dexter returned to Hampton?

"Sorry I'm late," said Mateo rolling his wheelchair up to her table. "Traffic's a nightmare coming out of the city."

"Oh – you're here," said Coqui, snapping from her thoughts of guns and murder.

He glanced down at Coqui's almost empty wine glass. "Glad to see it didn't slow you down any." His dark brown eyes danced with mischief: the small lines radiating outward from those eyes added a dash of experienced confidence.

"Mat-e-o, my man," said Jason. He slapped the flat of his hand against Mateo's back. "What'll it be?"

"Sam Adams," he answered. He looked across at Coqui. "Want to share some fried calamari?"

"Sure," said Coqui, "and you may as well bring me another glass of the La Crema."

"Will do," said Jason.

Coqui leaned back. "How was the game last night?"

"We won 82-68," said Mateo. "And I made twenty of those baskets." A large grin spread across his face as he reached in the leather bag beside him and removed an iPad. "Got the rest of the information you asked for." His large fingers swiped across the screen. "Everything

I could find on Sheri Barker. Not much, but did get a current address and phone number. I'll send that over to you."

"The other girl who was with Julie Ann and Deborah at the movies that night?" asked Coqui.

Mateo nodded.

"Thanks."

"For now, I thought you might find this interesting," He turned the iPad around for Coqui to see. "An old headshot of Dexter Sterling."

She enlarged the picture. "He was good-looking. I'll say that for him."

"But that's all he had going for him," said Mateo. "I only included the information in the first report that related to Earlene's case."

Jason set down the beer and the calamari. "" You guys ready to order?"

"Thanks, Jason, but we need a few more minutes," answered Mateo.

"Dexter had more trouble and run-ins than McDonald's has French fries," said Mateo. "He left a trail of used and abused women in his wake . . . put Shirley Finney in the hospital in 1975 . . . chased out of state by children of a woman he mooched off of in North Carolina in 1988 . . . sent Earlene into intensive care that same year –"

"I can't believe no one ever brought any charges against the man," interrupted Coqui.

"Not one," confirmed Mateo. He shook his head. "Guess they were glad to be rid of him."

Coqui speared a crispy ringlet and dunked it into Ricco's signature Bang-Bang Sauce. "So, who sent him packing in 1994?"

"For now, that's up in the air in my report. Got to do a little more digging. But I did find out that he lived in Florida for a while with a Hampton woman he'd lived with in 1975."

"Who was that?" asked Coqui.

"Cindy Sullivan." Mateo sipped his beer. "Her name is in the information I sent you."

Jason returned and brought Coqui another glass of wine.

"That alone makes the field wide open for suspects other than Earlene," said Coqui.

"But still only one with a confession and seen holding the murder weapon over the body at the scene of the crime," reminded Mateo.

"The gun is a problem," said Coqui.

"How so?" asked Mateo.

"Where did it come from and who did it belong to for starters," said Coqui reaching for more calamari.

"Point taken," said Mateo. "I'll see what else I can find out."

Jason reappeared.

Mateo looked across to Coqui. "You ready?"

She nodded. "I'll take the jicama salad and the grilled salmon."

"The same," said Mateo.

Jason scribbled down their orders on his pad and took their menus.

"Did you find out any more on the Watkins?" asked Coqui.

"Couldn't find a more respectable family . . . and Brenda Sue Watkins? Apparently, an angel sent by God." He reached into the bag again and pulled out a slip of paper. "Here's a list of the people they've helped over the years. They're also well connected with the local politicians and law enforcement agencies." Mateo sighed. "There's nothing shady about these people."

Mateo leaned forward. "Let it go."

"I don't know . . ." Coqui ran a hand across her chin. "That's the problem. Everything seems to be a little convenient for me." She gazed into Mateo's somber face. "If Dexter Sterling was so bad, why didn't Earlene at least go for a self-defense plea? Ms. Watkins hired the best attorney in Atlanta and —"

"And nothing," interrupted Mateo. "I hear what you're saying. *But* Earlene confessed, Coqui. She admitted to shooting Dexter." He sighed. "And evidently the attorney convinced her to do otherwise. It's all in the report I sent you."

"I know, I know," conceded Coqui. "Ms. Watkins told me today there's a storage unit with everything from the Thorntons' trailer. Julie Ann has the key."

"Want me to get it from her?" he asked.

Coqui shook her head no. "She's coming in tomorrow morning. I have some things I want to ask her." She didn't want to tell him that Julie Ann was beginning to look like a good prospect for the murderer. She decided to change the subject.

"Have you visited Raleigh?"

Mateo shook his head no. "I'm planning a little trip to his office tomorrow." He paused. "I've followed him the past few days. This afternoon he went with another woman to a hotel down in Buckhead."

Coqui smiled. "I hope you got pictures."

"Oh, ye-e-eah," sang Mateo. "Lots of them."

Chapter Nine

The following morning Coqui sat at her desk reading the reports Mateo had sent. Blue skies had replaced the rain, but the wind had picked up an occasional gust. Outside trees shivered and birds tucked themselves between branches, puffing out their feathers.

Coqui walked past the receptionist's desk. "Morning, Caroline," she greeted.

"Morning, Coqui." Caroline picked up a stack of mail. "Here you go."

"Thanks," said Coqui as she took the letters and walked toward her office.

After walking a few feet, she turned and called over her shoulder.

"I have a woman named Julie Ann Thornton coming around nine. Send her in."

"Will do," said Caroline.

Coqui entered her office, sat at her desk, and began thumbing through the envelopes. A small pink letter caught her attention: only her name was scribbled across the front . . . no postmark or any other identifying marks. Hopefully, it was a note of apology from Jenny.

She heard the front door open.

"Coqui?" a voice called out tentatively.

"In here, Julie Ann," she answered, laying down the envelope and rising from her seat.

"Good morning." Julie Ann Thornton smiled. She wore her slightly graying brown hair cut in a short bob. "Here's the key," she said as she slid a small, brown envelope across the desk.

"Thanks," said Coqui. She took the envelope and placed it beside the pink one.

"I can only imagine what condition that storage unit will be in," Julie Ann said. "No one's been there since the day the movers left. Once they rolled down that door, no one's opened it." She removed a piece of paper from her purse. "Here's the address. It's in Hampton."

Coqui nodded and took the paper. "Look, Julie Ann," she began. "I'm not sure I'm going to find anything new."

"I know." Julie Ann's lips trembled, and tears streamed from her eyes. If possible, her eyes were an even darker brown than Mateo's. She plucked a tissue from the box on Coqui's desk and dabbed her cheeks. Her voice was barely above a whisper. "I just want to give Mama one last fair chance."

Coqui managed a weak smile. "I'm doing my best."

"That's all I ask for." Julie Ann hesitated. "Is there anything else?"

Coqui shifted her weight from one foot to the other. "Actually, there is. Do you have a few minutes?"

"Sure," said Julie Ann.

Coqui motioned to the seat in front of her desk. "Could I get you a coffee or water?"

Julie Ann shook her head no, sat down, and crossed her legs, placing her shoulder bag in her lap.

Coqui sat down and opened the folder with Chief Holbrook's report in it.

"I'm trying to get a handle on what happened leading up to . . ." Coqui paused. "To Dexter's death." For now, she wanted to avoid the word "murder."

Julie Ann sat up straighter. "I'll tell you everything I can remember."

"Do you remember the names of the girls you went out with that night?"

Nodding her head, she answered, "Deborah Wood and Sheri Barker." A weak smile peeked through. "We were friends from elementary school through college."

"Have you remained in contact with either of them?" asked Coqui.

"I see Deborah when I stay overnight down in Hampton. She works at the Oak Tree Inn."

"I spoke with Deborah when I went down to talk with Blythe last Saturday night," said Coqui. "What about Sheri Barker?"

"Sheri called me for a while after the trial ended, but then we just lost touch." Julie Ann toyed with the handles on her purse. "I think Sheri felt uncomfortable about the whole thing."

"What about the movie? Do you remember what it was?" Coqui knew she was stalling for time, but she wanted to gently ease Julie Ann into that dark moment from her past.

"Braveheart," said Julie Ann. "Did you see it? With Mel Gibson"

"Wonderful movie." Coqui nodded. "Tell me . . . what do you remember up until you blacked out," she said. "From the time you left the theater until you saw Dexter dead?"

"When we got out of the movie, it had started to rain pretty hard. I said that I wanted to go home and pass on going to Shoney's for a burger. I'd coughed through much of the movie and my throat was getting scratchier. I could barely speak. All I wanted to do was get into my flannel pajamas and crawl into bed."

Coqui nodded in encouragement for her to go on.

"They dropped me off, said they hoped I'd feel better, and then I went inside the trailer. When I walked in, the first thing I noticed was the living room. There was a broken vase, and a couple of dinette chairs were turned over. There was also an empty bottle of whiskey on the coffee table. Then I heard shouting from the bedroom, and I knew Mama and Dexter were at it again."

"When you say 'again,' had Dexter moved back in with your mama?" asked Coqui.

"No, I hadn't seen him or heard Mama speak of him since he put her the hospital." She inhaled deeply. "But I'd never forgotten that horrible voice."

Tears formed in Julie Ann's eyes once more.

Coqui pulled more tissues from the box and extended them toward Julie Ann.

"Thanks." Julie Ann dried her eyes and then blew her nose. She cleared her throat and continued, "When I went into the bedroom, I saw them in an arm-lock and I ran to them, trying to break them apart."

"Did you notice the gun then?" Coqui interrupted.

"Yes, Mama was holding it and Dexter was trying to get it away. Mama told me to stay out of it and waved me to the side. Then Dexter pushed Mama while she wasn't looking . . . when she turned to talk to me."

"So, Dexter pushed your mama first?" Coqui was trying to cobble together a picture of how the events unfolded that night.

"Is that important?" asked Julie Ann.

"Maybe, maybe not, I'm just trying to put the pieces together," replied Coqui. "Go on."

"After he pushed Mama, I started hitting him with my fists, but then he pushed me hard, really hard." Her shoulders shook as her voice cracked. "That's all I remember. I must have hit my head because that's when I blacked out. When I woke up Mama was crying and had the gun in her hand, and Dexter was dead. Mama's hand was shaking so bad, I thought she might drop the gun, or it might go off again."

"What happened after you came to? Did you try to get up?"

"I started screaming, but," Julie Ann sighed. She sat frozen, as if in another world.

"Take your time," comforted Coqui.

"I remember seeing Miss Blythe come in."

"*That's* when Bylthe came in?" prodded Coqui.

"I think so . . . I don't know," Julie Ann cried into the soggy tissue. "I just remember her being there and her cradling Mama's head in her arms and the gun falling to the floor." Another flood of tears.

"It's okay," said Coqui.

Through gulps, Julie Ann said, "Then the next thing I remember is Miss Blythe and Mama taking me to the living room sofa. Mama held my hand and Miss Blythe put something under my nose. Smelling salts, I think."

"Okay, let's go back. When you went to stop the fight . . . before you fell and blacked out, do you remember if your mama still had the gun?" asked Coqui.

"She didn't, it flew out of her hand when Dexter hit her. I don't think either of them had it at that point."

Julie Ann tilted her head. "It's funny, I do remember one thing now that I'm thinking about it. When Dexter came at me . . . right before he pushed me, his eyes shifted, and he looked kind of shocked."

"Shocked?" repeated Coqui.

"Well, maybe not shocked . . . maybe more like surprised," she said. "I guess I've always thought it was because he'd caused Mama to hurt herself. I don't think he meant to hit her that hard. I mean she was crying and saying that he'd probably broken her arm again."

"Could be, but I don't get the impression that Dexter was the kind of man to have second thoughts about assaulting a woman."

"No." Julie Ann flushed. "No, he wasn't."

"What do you remember about the police arriving?" asked Coqui.

"Like I said, I'm kind of fuzzy about the details, but it seemed like only a few minutes before Chief Holbrook and his people got there." Tears streamed faster. "There were people all over the place. Mama was crying. Miss Blythe was holding her in her arms and screaming at Chief Holbrook – saying it was a blessing the devil had taken Dexter."

Julie Ann shuddered, reliving the memory of that night. She looked into Coqui's eyes and released a huge breath.

"I remember Mama telling me not to worry – Miss Brenda was sending someone to get me – that I'd be all right."

"Miss Brenda?" questioned Coqui.

"I think Blythe called her." Julie Ann nodded. "Yes, Miss Brenda and her driver, Donald Springfield, came to pick me up. Blythe walked me out to the car. Miss Brenda was sitting in the back seat."

"The trial only lasted two weeks, with just ten days between the murder and the conviction," said Coqui.

"That's right," confirmed Julie Ann. "The Watkins' family attorney took Mama's case."

"But two weeks? And no plea of self-defense?" Coqui questioned.

"Mama confessed and insisted she wanted the whole thing over. I think she was afraid the trial would attract too much attention." Julie Ann paused and then added, "Look, Coqui, I loved Mama, and she always saw that I had the best she could give me. That said, she had no taste when it came to men. And her morals didn't measure up to what polite society expected back then."

"You're saying that she just didn't want the bad publicity? Spending her life in jail was a good trade for a few weeks of scathing headlines?"

"Mama felt she was protecting me, and she knew Miss Brenda would do that and could provide me with a life that would never compare with what she had to offer."

"That's a big sacrifice," said Coqui.

"And that's why I want to clear her name if she was only trying to protect me."

Coqui studied her notes.

"Tell me if I've got this all straight. You came home from the movie and went into the trailer. The living room was a mess, things were all over the place. You heard a commotion from the bedroom, and when you entered, you saw your mama and Dexter struggling over a gun. You attempted to break up the fight, but your mama turned to face you and waved you away. That's when Dexter hit your mama. You went after Dexter again and began hitting him. Then he lunged at you, and as you went down you thought he looked surprised . . . distracted. Once you hit the floor, you blacked out."

"Oh, Coqui, I don't know. All I remember is my head crashing onto the floor and afterwards losing consciousness." She shook her head. "I'm so sorry."

Coqui placed her hand on Julie Ann's wrist. "You did great. That's all I ask."

She walked Julie Ann to the door and then returned to her desk. She glanced at the clock. She'd spent more time with Julie Ann than she thought. She needed to leave soon so she could be at Shirley Finney's house by one.

Coqui took the brown envelope from her desk, opened it, and then shoved the key down into her front jean's pocket.

Next, she picked up the pink envelope and opened it. On matching pink stationary there were five words in all caps:

STAY AWAY FROM EARLENE'S CASE.

Chapter Ten

For the third time in four days, Coqui found herself exiting I-75 and driving into Hampton. She drove down Georgia State Route 54, known to the locals as Roosevelt Highway. The road snaked its way beside a railroad track. The land was sparsely populated, farms and barns abandoned long ago. Rotted fences, ramshackle out-buildings, and overgrown fields were the only testaments to a lifestyle from decades past. According to her directions, Shirley Finney's home lay somewhere on this highway, ten miles from the Interstate.

A gust of wind blew a couple of plastic grocery bags along the shoulder – the threatening morning sky now meant to deliver on its promise of a nasty afternoon. Small clusters of houses cropped up now and then. Rusted appliances, cars up on blocks, and fallen trees were the only landscape attempts.

Coqui slowed down, looking for the addresses posted on each mailbox that lined the road. Checking her rearview mirror, she stopped and then made a right turn onto a driveway and followed it for about a quarter of a mile. Shirley Finney's house, removed from this community and placed in more prestigious surroundings, would earn a feature article in a cozy cottages' magazine.

Her house was white clapboard with evergreen shutters. There was a front porch complete with a swing, baskets of hanging ivy, and a tabby cat curled up on the top step. From her vantage point though, Coqui could see no welcoming mat, an omission suggesting maybe Shirley preferred her own company.

Marked-off sections of flowerbeds lay on both sides of the house, although they were now only a memory of summer past with winter fast approaching. Smiling gnomes and metal pinwheels greeted her as she drove closer.

As she parked her car, Coqui saw the front door ease open and Shirley emerge, walking in sock-feet across the porch to meet her on the sidewalk. Shirley smiled and lifted her hand. She was thin, close to anorexic with short blond hair.

Coqui got out of the car and walked toward her. "Hi, Shirley," she said, extending her hand.

"I see you found me," joked Shirley, and then turned and pointed to the cat, "And Matilda."

Matilda stared blankly at Coqui as if to say, "And you are interrupting my nap because?"

Another soft laugh from Shirley. "After Dexter, I decided that cats would be better companions than men."

"Much better," agreed Coqui as she took in Shirley's crooked nose, and three small scars left as a reminder of that trip to the hospital in 1975.

Coqui's stare didn't escape Shirley's notice. Unconsciously, her fingers brushed over the scars, and her eyes cast downward. "I think it's best we talk inside."

Coqui followed Shirley across the brick walkway the short way up to the front steps leading onto the porch and into the house. The inside was just as inviting as the outside. The floors were a dark wood with a few area rugs scattered around. Most everything was in neutral tones with an occasional pop of bright reds, yellows, and greens.

A whistling tea kettle halted Coqui's wandering eyes.

"I made some banana bread and can offer you some tea," said Shirley. "Or, something else to drink."

"Yes, to both," said Coqui. "Let me help."

"No," said Shirley, motioning her to sit. Then she turned and went into the kitchen area. "We can talk while I work."

"First, just tell me about Dexter," said Coqui, getting straight to the point in respect to Shirley's need to be at work in a couple of hours.

"At the time, I was embarrassed the night I had to go to the hospital," said Shirley. "Everybody knows everybody's business in Hampton and can't wait to be the first to share it. But once I got home, I got angry – more at myself than at Dexter.

"Shirley, you're not –"

Shirley held up a hand. "Let me finish. I said, 'At the time.'" She paused. "I felt I was responsible."

Coqui kept her mouth clamped, far too many women lived under this misconception.

I actually owe a lot to Dexter, in an odd way. He made me seek help . . . first at a domestic violence center. There I found a support group of women. A couple of those women invited me to their church. I'm over 60 years old now, but I know that I am worthwhile, that I am not a loser – I was hooking up with low-lifes because I thought that was the best I deserved."

Coqui remembered Mateo's notes on Shirley Finney – born to a fifteen-year-old girl and out-of-wedlock, with no idea who the father was. Abandoned, raised in a series of foster homes – too familiar a story, but this woman was living proof that there was always hope – with help and support.

"You're here about Julie Ann," said Shirley.

Coqui's face registered surprise. She'd told Shirley about a lot of things, but not that Julie Ann had hired her.

Shirley smiled. "As I said, news travels fast in Hampton, always has, always will."

"Then I assume you know she has hired me to clear her mama's name."

"Clear her name," Shirley snorted. "Ask me, the town should have erected a statue in her honor."

"So, you think she's really the murderer?" asked Coqui.

"To be honest, I don't think about it at all. I've had my own issues to deal with," she said flatly. She stared at Coqui. "Still deal with. But I'll be happy to tell you what I've heard."

Coqui listened as Shirley related the same scenario as every other person she'd spoken to over the last few days. When Shirley had finished, Coqui asked, "So, after the night of your attack, you never saw or heard from Dexter again?"

"Not true," replied Shirley.

"Really?" Coqui's attention sparked.

"You're right that I ever saw him again, but he did call me," said Shirley.

"When was this?"

"In 1988," answered Shirley. "A woman he had been mooching off of finally came to her senses; rather, her children made her come to her senses. They booted Dexter. He called me looking for a place to shack up."

"Guess he found that place with Earlene," said Coqui.

"Appears so. As I said, I'd built up some self-confidence and had a great support group to surround me. Earlene – not so much. She was an easy target and Dexter knew it. I also heard the woman's family threatened to expose him to the authorities for the aggressive scam artist he was."

Coqui pursed her lips. "Well, that certainly explains how he ended up back here in Hampton."

"I remember the year because that's when he sent Earlene to the hospital with two broken arms." Shirley glanced at the clock on the wall. "If there's nothing else, I need to get ready for work."

"I do have one more thing," said Coqui. "Dexter was murdered in 1994. Did he try to contact you then?"

"Uh, uh," said Shirley. "I told him off good when he called me in 1988. That's was the last I heard from him." She looked at the wall clock again. "I really gotta get going. I'm meeting the manager at Knollwood Village to plan a Halloween party for the residents."

"Gretchen Springfield?" Coqui broke in.

"How do you know her?"

"I met her when I went down to talk to Brenda Watkins."

"You talked with Miss Brenda?" asked Shirley.

Coqui nodded. "About Earlene."

"The world could use more people like Miss Brenda. She helped me start my new life here," she said. "Well, I hope I helped."

"You have." Coqui smiled, gathering her belongings and standing. "I'm beginning to add a few more pieces to the puzzle."

"Who else have you talked to?" asked Shirley.

Coqui listed the names of the people she'd contacted. "I'm headed over to the storage unit where all the contents from Earlene's trailer have been locked away for the past twenty-five years."

"Good luck," said Shirley. "Can't see what difference it would make now." Her face cast downward. "I heard about Earlene's death." She shook her head. "What a waste. Whatever you uncover, Coqui, Earlene Thornton was a good woman and Dexter Sterling was a bottom feeder. She deserved a lot better, and he deserved far, far worse."

Chapter Eleven

C oqui really didn't want to tackle the storage unit right now, but the thought of spending another night in Hampton or going home and returning tomorrow was even less appealing. She sighed and mentally prepped herself for the hours that lay ahead of her, hours of lifting and sorting through dusty, twenty-five-year-old, sad memories.

The storage unit facility was just a few miles from Shirley's place. Rain began pounding against the windshield, and a thick fog steamed up the inside, making it nearly impossible to see the road ahead of her. She slowed down, flipped on the defroster, and leaned forward in the seat, using her hand to wipe away the spot the defroster hadn't cleared.

The building with the storage unit Brenda Watkins had rented was right off Roosevelt Highway. Coqui wound her way to the group of numbers where the unit was located. At least parking would be easy. Hers was the only car in the lot. Coqui got out of the car and then raced through the lot to the tin roof covering the building. Following the numbers, she went down a row of units, easily finding number 29. She slid in the key and the lock popped opened. Raising the garage-like door, she entered.

A musty smell tickled her nose. Inside the unit was cold and dark, made even more so from the dismal, soggy weather. She listened to the driving rain on the tin roof, its sound deafening. Coqui felt along the wall for a switch and flipped on the lights. Overhead fluorescent bulbs flickered to life. She looked around: like Brenda Watkins had said, there really wasn't much. Coqui's stomach rumbled. While the banana bread was yummy, it wasn't enough to see her through the fast approaching dinner hour.

She walked over to a paltry collection of furniture that occupied one corner of the unit. Someone had placed a thin sheet over the top, but it had slid down to one side. An avocado-colored sofa, a Formica table with a couple of chairs, some lamps, and a recliner sat beside a twin bed with a white wicker headboard and a matching dresser and nightstand. The bedroom set looked as if it belonged to Julie Ann as a child.

A row of stacked boxes lined the opposite wall. Coqui sighed. May as well get started. She'd worn jeans and an old sweatshirt since she'd be spending the day on the floor, shuffling through belongings that hadn't been touched for twenty-five years.

Coqui placed her tote on the floor, and she removed a razor cutter from an inside pocket. She then walked over to the dinette table and placed the cutter on top. Coqui dragged the table beside the boxes. Grabbing one of the chairs, she dragged it over to the first stack of boxes. Testing the chair's sturdiness, she placed one foot on its seat, and then tentatively brought up the other foot. She slid off the top box and lowered it to the table.

None of the boxes were labeled, and considering Miss Brenda and Julie Ann's apathetic attitudes toward their belongings, the movers had probably tossed willy-nilly the Thorntons' things with no thought as to order or importance into the boxes. Using the cutter, she sliced through the packing tape. The tape was brittle and curled at its edges, making the box easy to open.

Inside she found an assortment of personal items she presumed had belonged to Earlene – an Atlanta Braves t-shirt, assorted shoes, a couple of purses, socks, underwear, and even the scarf she'd received that Christmas from Ms. Watkins. She also found some costume jewelry, memorabilia, and several plaques with bunnies holding flowers and a bright, chipper saying written in a squiggly style running across the bottoms. Coqui's heart squeezed. She couldn't imagine Earlene having many happy days.

Coqui replaced everything and closed the flaps. She carefully sorted through each box. They contained bathroom items, kitchen utensils, towels, and dishes. Books, photo albums, pictures that had probably hung on the wall, things common to most households, were the only keepsakes attesting to the Thorntons' meager existence in the trailer.

Coqui cleared the table and set the photo albums on top. She sat in the chair and began flipping through an album's pages. The album was neat and orderly. The pictures were mostly of Julie Ann, chronologically showing the short and sad life she'd had with her mother: Julie Ann as a baby, her first step, birthday pictures, school pictures, right up to the last Christmas they'd celebrated together in the trailer. She found the same picture Ms. Watkins had on her dresser . . . the picture of the three of them in their matching scarves. Coqui peeled away the picture from the page and set it aside.

Coqui thumbed through a second album until she came across a picture of Dexter and Earlene. She recognized Dexter from the headshot Mateo had shown her. This was a full shot of the two of them in bathing suits, probably taken in 1988. Dexter towered over her with an arm wrapped possessively around her waist. It was easy to see he was a former football player in the beginning stages of going to seed.

Lightning flashed outside and a deep rumble of thunder followed. The lights flickered and dimmed. Coqui stood and placed a fist in the small of her back. She only had one box to go. She sliced through its seal, pulling open the flaps. The box contained Julie Ann's personal items. There on top was the third scarf. Some stitching at the hem caught her eye: the initials "JAT." Julie Ann Thornton. Besides clothing and books, Coqui found a lunch-sized, brown paper sack. She peeked inside and saw partially used tubes of lipstick, a half-filled bottle of cologne, and an empty prescription bottle, probably from Julie Ann's bout with the stomach flu. As she returned the bag to the box, it ripped open and everything tumbled to the floor. Coqui gathered up the spilled things and threw them into the box.

Coqui began the task of resealing the boxes, setting Julie Ann's scarf aside. When she got to the box with Earlene's belongings, Coqui set aside her scarf as well. Perhaps Julie Ann might want one tangible memory from the trailer; maybe her mama's scarf might mean something to her, if not now, perhaps later. She laid it beside the picture she'd pulled from the albums. Coqui finished with the box and returned it to its proper place. As she walked back to the table, something crunched beneath her shoe. Raising her foot, she found the prescription bottle. It must have fallen unnoticed from the bag and rolled onto the floor. She leaned over and picked it up and read the label as she stood: "Take two tablets twice a day for bronchitis."

Coqui sat at the table and studied the bottle. Blythe's statement had said Julie Ann was home with a stomach flu. Even Julie Ann had said she'd coughed and had a sore throat that night. She sighed. While it seemed odd, did it really make a difference what Julie Ann had? Coqui sighed and stood. As she straightened, the lights went out. Even with the door open, everything was dark. She inched her way in the direction of the table to retrieve her phone, but she had only gotten a few feet when something slammed into the back of her head.

Chapter Twelve

Coqui awoke to a pounding in her head, a ringing in her ears, and a queasiness gripping her stomach. Everything remained dark, but now the door had been closed. She eased her way up to a sitting position, trying to find a spot on her body that didn't make her want to scream out in pain. Everything around her was literally pitch black; whoever had assaulted her had also taken the time to close the door.

Running her hands over the spot on her head where she'd been hit, and then over her face, she came back with a thick, sticky goo. She rubbed her fingers together: blood. Next, she ran her hands down each arm and leg, trying to take an assessment of how much she'd been injured. Slowly, she moved each body part, rotating her wrists and ankles, bending her elbows and knees. Nothing seemed to be broken.

Coqui sat there, collecting her thoughts. She remembered sitting at the Formica table looking at the prescription bottle, and then the lights going out. She had assumed it was the result of lightning hitting a transformer and knocking out the power. Then she'd felt the smack on the back of her head. Whoever hit her must have followed her there, watched her as she entered the storage unit to see what she was up to. Perhaps not liking what they saw, they shut off the circuit breaker unit before the attack.

Feeling the floor around her once more, she tried to get her bearings and figure out if she'd been left where she'd fallen or dragged to another area in the storage unit. She turned onto her hands and knees. As she did so, her stomach came back with violent flip-flops of protest. She sat back down in an effort to give her insides time to settle.

Coqui needed her phone, if in fact, her attacker had even left it behind. She had no clue what time it was or how long she'd been unconscious. She tried moving again, but the nausea pushed upward into her throat and she vomited uncontrollably.

After she'd finished, she wiped her mouth on her sleeve. Slowly, she extended her arms and spiraled them around her, her fingertips brushing against what she thought was one of the boxes. Gingerly, she paced her palms on the floor and inched her way toward the box.

Once there, she leaned back against the box and let the weakness wash over her and transport her into a deep sleep.

"COQUI," A VOICE SHOUTED. The door shook.

Coqui's eyes slit open. Her throat was parched, and her lips crusted, a sour taste coating her tongue and teeth. She ached all over.

"Coqui! Are you in there?"

Coqui turned her head. Daylight crept beneath the door.

"Mateo?" she rasped. "I'm in here."

She heard nothing from outside. She closed her eyes, her head splitting from the pain. She'd drifted in and out of sleep all night. Her thoughts were foggy and her memory becoming fragmented. A sound of rushing feet came closer.

"Can't you go any faster?" The voice was male, angry, and demanding. Mateo. Only now did she release a flood of tears of relief.

"Mateo." She tried one more time.

The door flew upward, and sunshine punched out the darkness. Covering her eyes with her hands, she soon heard rather than saw the people rushing toward her.

"I swear I had no idea anyone was in here," said another male voice, running a few feet behind Mateo.

Using a velocity he usually reserved for the basketball court, he wheeled toward her. Mateo shouted, "Call 9-1-1!" Then he leaned down beside Coqui. "What hurts?"

She squinted into his face: Mateo's eyes were breaming with tears. "I don't know . . . I mean . . . I don't think anything is broken," she croaked.

He raised her face gently, tilting it upward until it was inches from his, then he eased her face forward until he could see the back of her head. His fingers traced the wound.

"Ouch," cried Coqui, jerking away her head.

"Sorry," he said. "Any idea who did this to you?"

She shook her head no, and as she did a bolt of pain sliced through her, the nausea returning.

Mateo held her hands, tenderly but firmly. "Don't. Just stay quiet."

She could hear his ragged breathing.

"The ambulance is on its way," Mateo said.

Coqui couldn't let it go. "I think I found something," she blurted out. "I must be right. Someone is hiding something, Mateo."

Realizing his friend was back to her normal snoopy self, made Mateo breathe a sigh of relief and brought a slight smile to his lips. "Looks like you hit a nerve somewhere," he said.

The ambulance arrived and the paramedics did a preliminary evaluation.

"Nothing appears to be broken, and her vitals are normal, but we're taking her to the ER to do a thorough exam," explained a young man with a stethoscope around his neck.

"I'll follow behind," Mateo said. Then he leaned over and took Coqui's chin in his hand, "I'll see you there." He smiled. "Hang tough! I'll get your things."

"My car . . ."

"I'll send someone to get it and drive it to your place."

Coqui grabbed his hand as he was withdrawing it. "And get those two boxes over there," she said, extending a finger in the direction of the table. "One has two scarves lying across the top and the other has two photo albums in it."

"Not too injured to stop bossing me around," Mateo said to the paramedics as they were lifting Coqui onto a stretcher. Silently, he sent up a prayer of gratitude.

Chapter Thirteen

Coqui sat upright in her bed at home as Mateo plumped the pillows around her. "Watch it!" she complained.

"You're lucky you only came out with a concussion," scolded Mateo. He shook his head, his jaw clenched tightly. "You should see yourself. Your eyes are swollen almost shut and your entire body is covered in bruises."

"You saw my entire body?" barked Coqui.

"It's a figure of speech." Mateo rolled his eyes. "And besides, you'd never know the difference if I did."

"And what's that supposed to mean?" challenged Coqui.

"You were so out of it when I brought you home last night – "

"Last night? But I went to the hospital yesterday morning – "

"And by the time the doctors ran tests and decided to release you, it was after nine."

"Last night?" asked Coqui.

"Last night," confirmed Mateo.

Coqui her crossed arms and moaned. "I don't remember any of that."

"That's because the doctor had you heavily sedated."

Coqui peeked under the quilt. "Then how did I get into my pajamas?"

"Relax," reassured Mateo." I had Sue Ellen, one of the nurses from Just People, meet me here last night. She put you to bed and stayed with you until I could get back here this morning."

"Boy, I *was* dead to the world," grumbled Coqui. "I don't remember any of that."

"Too close to dead for my nerves." Mateo rolled into the bathroom, returning with a hand-held mirror.

Coqui studied her reflection and winced. She returned the mirror. "Take that thing away," she said, but this time more humbly.

"What were you thinking?" Mateo pulled out a folded piece of pink paper and handed it to Coqui. "And what exactly does this mean?"

She didn't need to read the note; she knew what it said: STAY AWAY FROM EARLENE'S CASE. "Where did you find this?" she demanded, shoving the paper back into Mateo's hands.

"It was inside your jean's pocket," he answered, gritting his teeth. He thumped the note with a finger. "Other than this tidbit of advice and being beaten senseless, have you received any other warnings?" His face was only inches from hers as he awaited an explanation.

Coqui raised herself up. "You went through my jeans?" she shrieked.

"Coqui!"

Coqui thought that Mateo sounded like a scolding parent, and deep down she knew he had every right. Her shoulders slumped as she clamped her lips tightly together.

Mateo rolled his chair across the floor, intentionally turning away from her gaze, afraid of what he might say. Suddenly, he spun around and spoke as sternly as he'd ever spoken to her. "And you never thought to include me in this warning?"

"I know," said Coqui softly. "It was dumb."

"Dumb?" Spittle flew from his mouth. He wiped a hand across his lips. "I think this surpasses dumb, Coqui." His face flamed. "I think 'idiotic' is a more accurate description." His voice rose louder with each syllable.

Coqui said nothing. What could she say? Mateo, as usual, was right.

He checked the time. "I need to meet Raleigh in an hour; otherwise, I wouldn't leave you," said Mateo. "Plus, Sue Ellen thinks you'll be fine. He pointed toward the nightstand, to a piece of paper lying next to Coqui's Bible. "There's her number if you need something."

Despite her aches and pains, she smiled. "You're showing Raleigh all the pictures?"

"I'm leaving him the complete set from the other three women besides Jenny," he said. "And keeping copies for our files."

"Are you showing them to Jenny?" asked Coqui.

Mateo shook his head no. "But I'm giving him twenty-four hours to make a clean break with her. After that, everybody gets copies of all the pictures . . . Jenny, his wife, and the other three women."

"Yikes!" Coqui rubbed her hands together. "Now you're talking. Let me go with you to deliver the pictures."

"That would be a strong and unchallenged 'no.'" said Mateo. "Besides, it will be my pleasure to see his reaction. Guys like him give the rest of us a bad name," said Mateo. Thoughts of the man he'd been before the accident flooded his mind. While he'd never come close to being an abuser, he had pridefully thought he was not only God's gift to women but to all he encountered.

"You can add Dexter Sterling's name to that list."

And but for the grace of God, thought Mateo, I could have still been that self-proud, arrogant man. Mateo lifted up a prayer of gratitude. His expression sobered. "And speaking of him, you are not to do anything else for forty-eight hours – doctor's orders." Then he added, "And that means not leaving this house."

Coqui nodded.

"And only with my help after that." Now his face softened, and he took her hand in his. "At my request . . . please. Whoever is behind all this means business."

"I'll call you after my visit with Raleigh." He leaned inward and kissed her cheek. "I made you a couple of sandwiches and put them in the refrigerator. You can get up, but please don't overdo it."

Coqui waited until she heard the door close, and then she eased from her bed. Her head felt some better, but she couldn't go anywhere now even if she wanted to. Her legs were stiff; her back was aching; and, her vision was still a bit on the blurry side.

She hobbled into the living room and peeked through the blinds. She watched as Mateo's truck rolled from the parking lot. Then she made her way over to the two boxes they'd brought home from the storage unit. She retrieved Earlene's two photo albums and carried them back to her bedroom, to the comfort of her bed.

Coqui spent the better part of the afternoon going through each photo. At the storage unit, she'd only flipped though the two albums – quickly, barely paying attention to either one of them in detail.

One album followed Julie Ann's life from birth until Earlene's arrest. The second one contained pictures from Earlene's early days. Like the other album, this one was chronologically ordered and neatly labeled. The photos were small, all black-and-whites, taken in the fifties, sixties, and then moving into the early seventies. Earlene had scribbled comments written in a peacock blue ink beside each one, her "i's" dotted with hearts. These photos were of Earlene and Blythe as girls. Pictures at family picnics, swimming at a lake, and several of them dressed up for various holidays. As Blythe had said, it appeared they had been inseparable. One showed them in miniskirts and white boots. The family resemblance was easy to recognize. Both were tiny and had long straight blond hair, large doe-like, blue eyes, and full lips displaying large grins and dimples.

After a few pages, Jack Thornton and Ricky Rawlins began appearing in photographs. There was one of the four of them. Ricky was only a few inches taller than Blythe and Jack was a head taller than Earlene. There was a page filled with snaps from their double wedding. Coqui realized after looking at the wedding pictures of Earlene and Jack that she'd mistaken the two men. It had been Jack who was the shorter of the two.

Jack and Earlene made a beautiful couple, almost like twins. Candid shots had captured the fair-haired couple smiling from ear-to-ear. If Blythe's memory could be trusted, Earlene had known she was pregnant already and Jack had been thrilled. The reason for their large, goofy grins? Below the wedding pictures, Earlene had written: August 16, 1975 – true love lasts forever.

Tears rolled down Coqui's cheeks . . . such a happy, hopeful pair. So many years before them. Only it hadn't turned out that way. Jack had been killed in the car accident three months later. Coqui continued to look through the album. It ended with pictures taken on Thanksgiving Day of Jack and Earlene, her with a growing tummy.

She went back to the first album, the one she'd looked at in the storage unit on Tuesday evening. It recorded Julie Ann as a baby until high school graduation. Coqui opened it. There weren't many photos, but Earlene had kept a meticulous record of Julie Ann's life, scrap-booking photos of special events and memorabilia from dance recitals, proms, and academic awards.

Two albums, two lives. The first one held black and white photos with girlish scrawlings by a young girl with a joyous and hope-filled heart. The second album was filled with color photos but seemed to be assembled by a woman who was just marking time.

Coqui's eyes grew heavy. She closed the album and pushed it to the side, and then she reached up to turn off the bedside lamp, her arm resisting the stretch. Exhausted, she drifted off with a sad eeriness created by a vision of a happy groom who never lived to see his baby girl.

Chapter Fourteen

A s Coqui opened her eyes, she saw faint silvers of light from the setting sun crisscross the carpet of her bedroom. Her head tensed and her neck tightened. Shifting upwards into a sitting position, she steadied herself on the side of the bed. The two photo albums had tumbled to the floor during her slumber. Their presence filled her with a renewed sadness at Earlene's life.

It was now Thursday afternoon, six days since Julie Ann Thornton had persuaded her to reopen her mama's case, and all Coqui really had to show for her efforts was a concussion and a battered and bruised body. She looked over to her phone lying at the foot of the bed and saw she had a missed call and a voicemail – both from Mateo. Better call him now or he'd soon call in the SWAT team, she thought. He answered on the first ring.

"Hi, it's me." Coqui yawned.

"You just now getting up?"

"Yup," she said. Mateo was driving. Coqui could hear the sounds of a siren and blaring car horns.

"Good. You needed a long rest."

"Yes, sir." Coqui mentally saluted. "Couldn't go anywhere even if I wanted to."

Mateo released a sigh of relief thinly blanketed with a forced chuckle.

"Have you met with Raleigh?" asked Coqui.

"Later. He had an appointment. Wanted to make it another time."

"Another time?" she interrupted, her voice elevating. "The nerve –"

"*But*, yes . . . calm down, I'm meeting with him one way or another tonight."

Satisfied with Mateo's response, she replied, "Let me know what happens." She ended the call and lay down her phone on the nightstand.

"May as well get up," she said aloud.

She shuffled her way to the bathroom, pain bolting through her body each inch of the way. She turned on the shower, and then she removed her pajamas and stepped in.

Coqui breathed in deeply. The hot, steamy water drenched away the grime and stench from her night in the storage unit and later at the hospital. It also seemed to loosen her stiff body parts. Being clean absolutely made a world of difference – she was steeled with a new resolve to tackle this case head on. While she felt she hadn't come any closer to clearing Earlene's name, she must be on to something. Otherwise, why was she being warned off? She was more determined to probe deeper – that her hunch must be right. That resolve was now backed with a motivation to find out who her attacker was. Having a fresh perspective and a clear mind coupled with the new information would send her in a more focused direction. She also had a huge rumbling in her stomach that refocused that resolve toward the kitchen.

Coqui opened the refrigerator and stared at the anemic-looking turkey sandwiches Mateo had so thoughtfully prepared. She shook her head. What she needed was power food. Within the hour, she'd eaten the better part of a large, Meat-Lovers Pizza that she'd had delivered. She refilled her water bottle, and then she settled in at the table to begin her evening.

Opening her laptop, she typed in Hampton High School 1974-75 yearbook. That was the year that they'd all been seniors. The class had been small, their pictures only taking up a few pages. She passed pictures of Earlene, Jack, and Ricky . . . but no Blythe. Then Coqui remembered she'd been a year younger than the others. Blythe wouldn't have graduated until the following year. Coqui flipped to the section with the teachers and looked at Brenda. Poor Brenda, even as a young woman, she'd been more than just plain. She was downright unattractive. Her expression was serious and difficult to read, very much looking the part of a forlorn schoolmarm.

Coqui turned back to the graduating class and noticed a student named Donald Springfield. That was Gretchen's dad, the man who lived upstairs with Brenda, the one whose family Brenda had helped during their hard times. She made a note to talk with Gretchen to find out more about her family's involvement with the Watkins.

Coqui leaned back. She didn't realize they had all gone to school together. Since they were all the same age, it did make sense. If you'd grown up in Hampton, you would have to have gone to Hampton High. She sighed. Did that even make a difference? Of course, everyone in Hampton knew each other . . . and each other's business according to Shirley Finney.

Coqui looked at her notes. 1975 was also the year Dexter had come to Hampton for the first time. According to Blythe, he'd worked his way through many women. Coqui took out a pencil and jotted down the names of the girls in the senior and junior classes. Maybe if any of them were still around, they could give her added information on the Hampton community at that time, and insight into Dexter Sterling. There had to have been other women he'd been involved with, and touching base with them might lead to a clue . . . a bit of information that might highlight a new suspect or maybe give her a clue as to who was after her. Maybe . . . or just wasted time?

She moved to the pages with photos of clubs and activities. Earlene and Blythe had been in Future Homemakers of America, but that was it for their extracurricular activities. Neither Ricky nor Jack had participated in sports. The school had a winning football team that year. Coqui smiled when she came to the page with the Homecoming Celebration. It was the only color picture in the entire yearbook. Jack and Earlene had been the King and Queen. They stood on a high platform surrounded by the Homecoming Court. The girls' dresses were a rainbow of colors with the escort of each wearing a matching color shirt. Earlene and Jack wore a baby blue complimenting their eyes.

Coqui looked through the pages one more time, looking for females she thought may have crossed paths with Dexter. She tossed aside the pencil and rubbed her forehead. Did she really need more women to attest to this man's sleaziness? No matter who she might choose to talk to, they would all most likely agree: Dexter Sterling was a worthless user.

Coqui closed the site with the yearbook and placed both her elbows on the table. The most important thing she needed to know was Dexter's time frame in Hampton, focusing on those she knew he had come into contact with there, and confirm his whereabouts in Hampton during that time. He had arrived in the spring of 1975 and had left abruptly at the end of summer in that same year. She now knew that he left to escape the law for putting Shirley Finney in the hospital. Then, after that, at some point later he'd landed with a woman in North Carolina.

Coqui opened the file on Vivian McAlister. She was that woman. Vivian was widowed at the of age forty-five and was a few years older than Dexter. Her husband had been an extremely successful brain surgeon. Ironically, he'd died of an undetected, malignant brain tumor. He'd left her a beautiful house in the mountains and a well-appointed lifestyle. She was perfect picking for a man like Dexter. He got by with it for a while, but soon her children wised up and sent him packing with the threat of legal proceedings. So, in 1988 he took refuge in Hampton.

Upon arrival, he'd called Shirley, but by that time she'd come to her senses and would have no part of him. He'd contacted Earlene. He'd found shelter with her. According to her conversation with Blythe on their first meeting, Dexter seemed to have settled down for a while. Maybe being hunted by the law had motivated him to cool his heels. Then the rage built up once again and he put Earlene into the hospital and fled Hampton for the second time.

There wasn't much in Mateo's notes about Dexter's whereabouts until he reunited with the woman he'd lived with for a while in Hampton in the spring of 1975. Her name was Cindy Sullivan and Mateo had provided a Florida address and phone number. Coqui looked at the clock. It was after eleven . . . too late to call anyone at this hour. All phone calls would have to wait until tomorrow. Besides, people and times were becoming blurred. Coqui brought out a clean notecard and tried to put people and dates into some sort of order:

1946 – Brenda was born

1950 – Dexter was born

1956 – Earlene, Jack, and Ricky were born

1957 – Blythe was born

1975 – Dexter came to Hampton for the first time and at some point, moved in with Cindy Sullivan that spring

1975 – Earlene, Jack, and Ricky graduated from Hampton High, where Brenda Watkins was a teacher

1975 – that summer Earlene found out she was pregnant, and she and Jack married; Blythe and Ricky married also

1975 – Dexter put Shirley into the hospital, and he left Hampton

1975 – Jack was killed in an automobile accident the weekend after Thanksgiving

1976 – Julie Ann was born

1988 – Dexter left Vivian McAlister in North Carolina because her children threatened legal action and he returned to Hampton

1988 – Dexter contacted Shirley; he moved in with Earlene

1988 – Dexter sent Earlene to the hospital and he left Hampton for the second time

1988 – Julie Ann moved in with Brenda Watkins

1994 – Dexter returned to Hampton

1994 – Dexter was murdered

1995 – Earlene was sentenced to prison

Coqui studied her timeline. She needed to talk to Vivian McAlister and Cindy Sullivan about their relationships with Dexter. Also, she wanted to learn at what point Cindy and Dexter had reconnected and what happened to him during the years 1988 until they got back together. Most important, Coqui needed to know why Dexter had returned to Hampton, in particular to Earlene, in 1994. In her gut, she felt that was the reason for his death.

Chapter Fifteen

The morning sun moved across Coqui's shoulders and coaxed her from a deep slumber. She heard her phone ringing and sat up. Pain shot through her body. Wincing aloud, she grabbed the phone from the bedside table and collapsed backwards into her pillow.

"Good morning," she groaned. The old aches and pains that had subsided last night seemed to have returned with a vengeance.

Mateo laughed. "Doesn't sound too good on your end."

Coqui chose to ignore his buoyant mood. "How did it go with Raleigh last night?" she asked.

"I don't think we'll have any more trouble from him," assured Mateo.

"When is he talking to Jenny?"

"He promised he'd take care of that today," he said. "You think Jenny will call you?"

"We'll see." She sighed. "I hope so; I'll give her a few days and then I'll reach out if I haven't heard from her."

"How are you feeling today?" asked Mateo.

"Haven't gotten up yet, but I plan to move around some," she said. "I can't just lie around in bed all day. I'll go nuts."

"Remember what the doctor said," he reminded her. "Rest for forty-eight hours." Then he added, "And that means forty-eight, not twenty-four."

"I've got it already. Okay?"

Mateo dismissed her rotten mood and changed the subject. "I've got to be at the Titans' practice this morning otherwise I'd drop by."

"I'm fine," reiterated Coqui. "Don't change your plans because of me."

"If we win the next game, the team will advance to the District Playoffs."

"When's the game?"

"Tomorrow morning."

"I'll be there," said Coqui.

Mateo hesitated. "The doctor *recommended* forty-eight hours, but you may need extra time."

"I meant I'll be there in spirit." Coqui rolled her eyes.

He paused and then with a catch in his voice he proceeded, "Coqui, you were hit pretty hard."

"Okay," she interrupted. "I told you I'd take it easy." Irritation colored her tone. "Give the Titans my best."

Coqui laid the phone beside her on the bed, and then slowly sat up. After a couple of minutes, she stood. Her head was light and swimming, but nothing compared to what it had felt like yesterday morning, and the nausea seemed to have disappeared. She felt a little hungry even after her pizza-fest the previous meal. At least her appetite was returning – good sign.

She wobbled her way toward the kitchen to make some breakfast. Her lower back throbbed, and her knees were stiff. She looked down: well, no wonder. They were swollen into black and deep purple lumps. She must have gone down on all fours when she'd been hit.

While her coffee brewed, she popped a slice of bread into the toaster. She grabbed a jar of peanut butter from the pantry and unscrewed its lid. Digging in a finger, she scooped up a dollop, shoved it into her mouth, and licked her finger clean. She ate her peanut butter and strawberry toast at the kitchen counter and let her mind clear. When she'd finished eating, she rinsed off the knife and plate and placed them in the dishwasher. She made a second cup of coffee and took it to the table. Then she retrieved her laptop from the bedroom, along with all her notes. Somewhere in the night her laptop had run out of battery. Coqui rummaged around in her tote for a cord and then plugged it in.

While she waited for the laptop to start, she thought about what she needed to do first. She wanted to talk to Vivian McAlister, the woman from North Carolina, and Cindy Sullivan, the Hampton woman now living in Florida with whom Dexter had rekindled a relationship. When her laptop sprang to life, she opened her email. The only one that interested her was the one from Mateo. He had sent her a little more information on Dexter Sterling. As she read, she found that most of the new things were traffic violations and parking tickets.

Picking up her phone, she dialed Vivian McAlister. Coqui introduced herself and explained why she was calling. Vivian was open to talking to her about her relationship with Dexter.

"He was never abusive with me," said Vivian.

"You were never aware of any of his past issues?" asked Coqui.

"Huh-huh," she said. "Not until my children told me about them." Vivian was quiet for a moment before she continued. "I'm pretty sure the reason for his good behavior was because of his access to my money." She laughed. "That man sure did love the good life. He just didn't want to work for it."

Then Vivian told of the expensive bottles of wine he'd ordered, the extravagant trips they'd taken, and the fine restaurants they'd frequented. While it was all very enlightening, none of the stories were adding anything to her investigation into the man's murder.

Finally, Vivian slowed down. "That's about it, I guess. Hope I've helped."

"Yes, tremendously," said Coqui making it sound more valuable than it was. "And thank you again for talking with me."

Coqui moved next to Cindy Sullivan. She didn't answer, so Coqui left a voicemail asking her to return the call. Coqui moved back to her computer and pulled up the Hampton High School website. She followed the menu to the 1974-75 yearbook section and opened it. Once more she looked at its pages – still no new insights. She laughed as she wondered what Blythe had looked like in her senior picture. She opened the 1975-76 yearbook and looked for Blythe, but there was no photo. Not surprising, thought Coqui. Blythe would have been a married woman by then and had chosen not to return to school. Coqui couldn't imagine a high school diploma would have meant much to her.

Coqui moved to the faculty section. Perhaps Brenda Watkins would have made a better picture that year. No picture of her either. Two other teachers' names were listed below with the words "not pictured" beside them. No mention of Brenda Watkins. Odd, where was she that year? Then Coqui looked at all the years Brenda Watkins had taught, and there was a picture of her for each year in the faculty section. Coqui sat back, took up her phone, and called Gretchen Springfield.

"Good afternoon, Knollwood Village," answered Gretchen.

"Gretchen, Coqui. Say, I have a question for you if you have a minute," said Coqui.

"Sure, hope I have an answer," she responded.

"I was going through some Hampton High yearbooks, and I noticed Brenda Watkins didn't teach the 1975-76 school year. Do you by any chance know where she was that year?"

"Let me think." There was a pause. "Not sure of the year but Miss Brenda did spend a year taking care of her dad's sister who was bed-ridden at home. She'd been in an automobile accident and the Watkins sent Miss Brenda to help her recuperate."

"That would make sense," Coqui said.

"The Watkins were suspicious of doctors and hospitals . . . like I said, Miss Brenda was always helping someone. Anything else?"

"No, you've been great. Thanks."

Coqui lay down the phone. She supposed that made sense. She shook her head. As much sense as anything else was making. Without too much to do at the moment, except wait for Cindy Sullivan to return her call, Coqui decided to gather up some clothes for the cleaners. She especially wanted to take in the outfit she'd worn at the storage unit and the hospital.

Coqui took the clothes to the front door and placed them on a chair. The two boxes she'd brought to give to Julie Ann were sitting beside the chair. May as well get the photo albums she'd looked at last night and place them in the boxes. Perhaps she and Mateo could drop the boxes by Julie Ann's house tomorrow after the Titans' morning game.

She leaned over and pulled back the flap on a box. There on top was the picture of Earlene, Julie Ann, and Brenda in their matching scarves. It was taken in front of the fireplace at the Watkins' estate. Coqui remembered seeing this setting from her visit to Knollwood Village. All three women wore large grins. Brenda and Julie Ann stood on either side with Earlene in the middle. At Christmas of 1993, Julie Ann was eighteen – that would have made Earlene thirty-six. Coqui's heart squeezed, so young and so much sadness . . . and so much more sadness in her immediate future.

As Coqui returned the photo albums to the box, she saw another scarf. She remembered placing the other scarf in the box as well. Finding it, she placed the two together. The scarves had been wadded up, and both reeked of the noxious mustiness things acquire from being packed away for so many years. Maybe she'd drop them off by the cleaners before she took the boxes to Julie Ann.

Coqui stood and placed the scarves on the stack of clothes she had ready to drop off at the cleaners. As she placed the scarves on the top of the pile of clothes, one slid onto the floor with the initials exposed at the corner. As she bent over to pick it up, she noticed "BSW." She looked at the other scarf. "JAT" was stitched into its corner.

Why would Brenda's scarf be in Earlene's trailer if she'd never been there? And if she had been to the trailer, why would she lie about it? Of course, Coqui reasoned, maybe Earlene had mistakenly taken Brenda's scarf that night when she went back home. Maybe? She shook her head and turned . . . much too quickly. Dizziness forced her to place her hands on the wall and steady herself. She gritted her teeth as pain shot through her left side. This was not what she wanted. She was in no shape to accomplish much of anything on her own – at least outside these walls. She went to the kitchen and grabbed the bottle of pain pills, shaking two into the palm of her hand. She downed them with water. Then she made her way to the sofa and curled up under a thick afghan.

Chapter Sixteen

Coqui awoke and glanced at the clock. She'd slept for about an hour. While somewhat groggy, the cat nap had renewed her sagging energy. The room was chilly when she emerged from the cover. She went into the kitchen and made a cup of coffee. While her coffee brewed, she checked her phone – no voicemail or missed call from anyone: Coqui had hoped to hear from Cindy Sullivan by now.

When her coffee finished, Coqui returned to the table and eased down in front of her laptop. Going back to the Hampton High's website, she clicked the yearbook section. From what she could tell, Brenda Watkins began teaching English in the 1969-70 school year and stopped at the end of 1988-89, only missing the 1975-76 school year. The year Brenda Watkins had retired would have coincided with the time she began caring for Julie Ann when Dexter had put her mama in the hospital.

Coqui stood and walked slowly to her bedroom, picking up the pile of notecards she'd reviewed last night. Coqui sat down at the table once more and spread out the cards in front of her. She began with the stack of suspects and reviewed what she'd written.

Earlene. She'd confessed to the murder. She had a motive (Dexter's abuse), opportunity (he was in her trailer at the time he was murdered), and there was an eyewitness (Julie Ann).

Coqui paused and stared ahead. She now felt Julie Ann was not a reliable witness. Since she'd blacked out for the actual murder, Julie

Ann was more of an after-the-fact witness. And while she'd seen no reason to doubt Earlene's confession, Coqui was beginning to feel more and more that Earlene was not Dexter Sterling's murderer. All those little things that had lined up so perfectly were now becoming loose and falling apart. The gun and the quick trial were becoming more and more problematic. There had to be an explanation as to why Earlene's were the only fingerprints on the murder weapon, and why there had been such a speedy trial with no apparent attempt to go for a self-defense plea. Coqui sensed the answers to those two problems would point to Earlene's innocence. She set Earlene's card aside and lifted up the next one.

Julie Ann. She was becoming a stronger possibility. If it had been an accident and she didn't remember what she'd done once she came to, then it was plausible she could have shot Dexter as she was falling to the floor, and the murder scene been set up so that Julie Ann would remember it that way. Coqui believed if the scene had been arranged, it wouldn't have been to Julie Ann's knowledge. She was reporting what she saw and believed to be true, and that was making Julie Ann a more likely suspect than Earlene.

Coqui could understand Earlene wanting to protect her daughter, but again, why not go for a self-defense plea for Julie Ann? Everyone hated the man. Then another thought wedged its way in. Perhaps Dexter's death hadn't been self-defense after all. Maybe Earlene had intended to kill him all along, and Julie Ann came home early requiring a new plan. Maybe Dexter had called Earlene, and she'd invited him over . . . laying a trap to murder him.

Coqui shook her head. Shirley Finney had said that Dexter had called in 1988 looking for a place to crash for a few days while he decided how to settle his current situation. That had been when he'd been in the mess with Vivian McAlister. After Shirley turned him down, Earlene had taken him in. That decision had landed her in the hospital for a month. Dexter's return in 1994 had been different. He'd not tried Shirley at all. Coqui contemplated the situation. Would he have had the nerve to call Earlene leaving town the way he did? Of course he would, thought Coqui. Men like him knew no shame. She had assumed Dexter was running away from a nasty situation in 1994 as well. What if he had returned to Hampton for a reason? And that reason had caused him to call Earlene, bypassing Shirley.

Coqui picked up Shirley Finney's card and placed it to the side. She felt she could rule her out as a suspect for the time being. As she reached for Blythe's card, her phone rang: Cindy Sullivan. Coqui placed the notecards to the side.

"Cindy, thank you for calling me back," said Coqui, explaining the reason for her message. She reached for a pen and a small legal pad.

"Sure, I'll tell you what I can remember." Cindy laughed. "I guess Dexter Sterling is going to keep turning up in my life until the day I die."

"Let's hope not," said Coqui. "Let's start with when you first met Dexter."

"Spring of 1975 . . . but, you know that already."

"How did you meet?" What was your relationship like?" Coqui prodded.

"I'd been out of nursing school for about a year and had gone to work at a clinic on the outskirts of Hampton. Back then there were a lot of families needing medical attention but didn't trust large hospitals or preferred coming to a closer facility. One night after my shift, I went with some friends for a drink . . . to wind down. I met Dexter in the bar that night, and we hooked up." Cindy stopped. "That was over forty years ago. I can't recall the name of the bar."

"Probably not important," said Coqui. "Go on."

"We dated for a couple of weeks and then he moved in." She took a breath and continued, "Considering his past, we had a peaceful coexistence."

"Did he leave you for Shirley Finney?"

"Oh, no – Dexter didn't dump me. I'm the one who gave him the boot."

That surprised her. Coqui had just assumed he'd left Cindy for greener pastures. "Any particular reason?" Coqui asked.

"Dexter was a two-timing bottom-feeder. I knew that, and I knew it would only be a matter of time. He was becoming more distant, less interested in me. He began acting strange, though." Cindy's voice trailed off.

"What do you mean strange?" Coqui didn't want Cindy to lose that train of thought.

"At the time I thought he must have been making some money on the side," she said and then added quickly, "not that I ever saw any of it."

"What made you think he had money?" asked Coqui.

"He bought a new car and started wearing expensive clothes and cologne. Things like that."

"He bought a new car and started wearing expensive clothes and cologne?" questioned Coqui, thinking of the information Mateo had collected on him. She'd never seen any mention of jobs. "I didn't know he ever worked."

"Whatever it was, I don't think it was legit. Like I said, I never saw or heard anything about that money. As far as our relationship, my place was becoming just somewhere to hang his hat."

"Do you know where he went from there?" asked Coqui.

"Back to the Alamo Plaza. I didn't really keep up with him, but I did hear about the police being called over there a few times."

"Is that where he beat up Shirley Finney?"

"Yes, and that was the last I heard of Dexter Sterling until 1993."

"And in 1993 you two just picked up where you'd left off in 1975?" Coqui questioned.

Cindy sighed. "Look, in some ways Dexter and I were two of a kind. I've never married. I'm in and out of relationships as the mood suits me. I'm kind of a nicer, gentler female version of Dexter, only I don't use people. It's just that a permanent commitment is not for me."

"So, who ended the last relationship?"

"Dexter and I took up in the fall of 1993 and he stayed for a little over a year. One day I came home from work and he was gone."

"Do you know why?" asked Coqui.

"Dexter Sterling didn't need a reason; he came and went as he pleased." Then Cindy added, "I was a little surprised at his sudden departure. The night before, we had dinner at an upscale restaurant, complete with an expensive bottle of wine. We even bought a second bottle and brought it home . . . polished it off as well. We spent the night laughing, talking about Hampton, the people and their lives there. We got out yearbooks and looked through them. I continued to buy one every year after I graduated. It was a fun way to keep up with locals, especially after I moved away."

"So, when did you leave Hampton?" asked Coqui.

"Summer of 1976. I was getting tired of the small-town life . . . everybody knowing everybody else's business. Also, I longed for a more pleasant climate."

"Did you know Brenda Watkins and Earlene Thornton?"

"Knew the Watkins by reputation only. Miss Brenda was my English teacher. I went to school with Earlene and Jack. I was there the night their baby was born. As a matter of fact, I delivered Julie Ann."

Coqui sat up straight. "You were there?"

"I was still working at the clinic at the time. Earlene went into pre-mature labor and Blythe brought her in. Such a tiny little thing. I didn't think the baby would last the night. I was surprised when I heard that she'd lived."

"You didn't stay the whole night?"

"I sat with them for a while, the baby sleeping in an incubator, Earlene in a rocking chair close by. But, yes, I left. Another patient came in – I think it was the Watkins – probably Mr. Watkins, he had heart trouble."

"Why do you think it was the Watkins? Did you see them?" asked Coqui.

"No," admitted Cindy. "I saw their car in the parking lot as I left the clinic. The doctor with them told me he would stay with Earlene and the baby so I could go home."

Neither spoke. It was Cindy who broke the silence.

"I hope something I've said helps with your investigation, although I'm not sure what difference it would make now . . . poor Earlene . . . and poor Julie Ann."

"Did Dexter ever talk about what he did when he left Hampton in 1988 until you two reconnected?" asked Coqui.

"Same old, same old. Moved from one woman to the next, looking for the good life."

"Did he mention anyone who might have seemed special?"

"You've got to be kidding!" she exclaimed. "All Dexter Sterling ever wanted was to be taken *care of* . . . he never *cared for* anyone."

After her conversation with Cindy, Coqui studied her timeline, and then she reread all Mateo's files. She poured over the notes she'd taken, beginning with her talk with Blythe Rawlins a week ago. So much information in fact, that she felt like she was overlooking something important. A detail that would make her see things in a different light. Consumed by mental exhaustion and physical fatigue, Coqui moved from her seat at the table and moved to her bathroom to get ready for bed.

Sleep came easily and took her deep into the night, but unfortunately, it did not remain. In the wee hours of predawn Saturday, Coqui awoke to the vision of the happy Homecoming King and Queen in their matching blue attire.

Coqui's brain whirred. She went to her laptop, pulled up the Homecoming picture of Jack and Earlene, and printed it. Coqui looked at the smiling couple: she needed to return to Knollwood Village, and she couldn't wait until after the Titans' game.

Chapter Seventeen

At least she'd listened to Mateo on one count, Coqui reasoned to herself: she'd called a car service to take her to Hampton this morning rather than drive herself. He could come down after the Titans' game. After all, she felt much better this morning, and it was just over forty-eight hours. That meant she'd followed the doctor's orders.

Coqui got out of the car and told the driver he could leave. She'd left Mateo a voicemail to pick her up, or she could schedule another car service to take her home. As she walked toward the stairs, she patted the side of her tote to feel the umbrella she would need for her cover story for her return visit to talk to Gretchen. She took a deep breath as she entered the doors to Knollwood Village. Gretchen was sitting at her desk, busy with a pile of folders stacked in front of her.

"Coqui, surprised to see you." She smiled, but her tone was defensive. "Miss Brenda's not having a good day."

The element of surprise was also a part of Coqui's plan . . . no time for Gretchen to make up a story to answer her questions. Coqui held up her hands. "No, no . . . not here to bother her," she reassured Gretchen. "I'm back in Hampton to tie up some loose ends."

"Oh?" Gretchen's eyes widened with a renewed interest as she moved from behind her desk. "And Knollwood Village has those loose ends?" She emphasized her last words.

"No loose ends here, but I do need to talk to a couple of other people in Hampton." Coqui replied. "I came by because I've misplaced my umbrella and I thought I might have left it here. Mind if I look by the coat hooks?" No need to let Gretchen or Miss Brenda know that they were exactly the loose ends that needed tying up.

"No one's turned in any stray umbrellas," Gretchen said.

"I probably didn't leave it here, but thought since I was down this way, I'd stop by just to make sure . . . if it's no trouble."

Gretchen smiled, her expression saying she wasn't sure if she believed Coqui. "Of course." She moved closer.

"No need to bother. I see you've got work to do," said Coqui pointing to the papers spread across Gretchen's desk. "I remember where the coats are." She quickly added, "It'll just take a second and then I'll be on my way – won't bother you again."

Gretchen nodded. "I'll go with you."

Coqui and Gretchen made their way to the back of the kitchen to where all the coats were hanging.

Right there, where she'd seen it when she collected her jacket the other day was the third scarf. Coqui made a show of looking for the umbrella and purposely knocked down the scarf and turned over its end: EDT. Earlene Davis Thornton. She smoothed down the scarf, and while she was bent over, she slid the umbrella from her tote.

"Found it!" she said holding up the umbrella as she passed Gretchen. "Thanks, again."

Gretchen held up two hands. "Are you in a rush?"

"Not at all," said Coqui.

"Why don't you join me for a cup of coffee in my office," offered Gretchen.

"Sure." Coqui's heart leaped. This couldn't be working out better for her. The difficult part of her plan had been how to start a conversation with Gretchen without raising her suspicions at the same time.

Coqui followed Gretchen into her office and then waited while she went for the coffee. Minutes later, she returned with two steaming mugs and placed one in front of Coqui.

"Would you mind sharing with me why you're still talking to people?" asked Gretchen.

"Things just aren't adding up," replied Coqui.

"But everyone knows that Earlene made a full confession, went to trial, and was sentenced to prison," said Gretchen.

"And on the surface, that works well." Coqui shifted in her chair. "It works too well. And as you said, everyone was happy with the outcome."

"And that's a problem?" Gretchen leaned back in her chair, tilted her head to one side, and shrugged her shoulders.

"Actually, Gretchen, that is the problem." Coqui set down her cup before continuing. "Julie Ann comes to as Blythe comes into the room – presumably from hearing a scream and sees her mama with the murder weapon in her hand and then listens as Earlene confesses to Dexter's death. It's at this point that Blythe calls Chief Holbrook. Then she takes Earlene and Julie Ann to the sofa in the living room to wait for Holbrook. Now there are four people to hear the confession."

"So, where's the problem?" asked Gretchen.

"Oh, there are multiple problems, but the first one that bothered me was that with all the Watkins' money, I'm sure they hired a first-rate attorney. So, why didn't he go for a self-defense plea."

Gretchen pursed her lips but remained quiet.

"At first I thought that Earlene just didn't want all the publicity from an extended trial." Coqui shook her head. "But why? I even considered the possibility that Julie Ann shot Dexter during the struggle."

"Julie Ann?" Gretchen laughed, a little too loudly and a little too forced. "Really, Coqui. Your mind has been busy, especially for someone with a head injury. Maybe that's what's been giving you these wild thoughts."

Coqui smiled. "Yes, I admit that was foolish thinking on my part. You see, if Julie Ann had shot Dexter in the middle of the struggle, that would still be self-defense."

"I'm listening," said Gretchen.

"A thirty-six-year-old woman would have to have a bigger reason to trade away the rest of her life in prison."

"And did you uncover that deep, dark secret from Earlene's past?"

"I think I have." Coqui nodded. She could feel a tiredness welling inside. Maybe waiting for Mateo to come with her would have been a better idea. She shook her head. "And Miss Brenda, too."

"Miss Brenda?"

"When I first visited Miss Brenda's room, I saw the picture of the three of them in front of the fireplace here at the estate."

Gretchen shrugged. "That was the night Miss Brenda gave them the scarves."

"Right, and Miss Brenda made a point of saying she'd never been in Earlene's trailer." Coqui leaned forward. "Yet when I went through the storage unit, I found a scarf in a box of Earlene's things – only it had the initials 'BSW' at the hem."

"So?" objected Gretchen. Her impatience was surfacing.

"So, when I checked the scarves here a minute ago, the scarf here had 'EDT' – Earlene's initials. That picture was taken two days before Dexter died. How did Miss Brenda's scarf get mixed in with the things taken from Earlene's trailer?"

Gretchen shrugged. "Perhaps Earlene wore home the wrong scarf that night."

"Perhaps not," corrected Coqui.

"Guess we'll never know," said Gretchen. "Guess that loose end will never be tied up."

"Unfortunately, that's not the only loose end," persisted Coqui.

"How so?"

"Well, when I looked through the other boxes from the trailer, I discovered several more *loose ends*."

"Continue," said Gretchen.

"I found a prescription bottle from Julie Ann's stomach bug, as well," said Coqui.

"You've been a busy girl. What does that have to do with anything?"

"It was a prescription for bronchitis."

"Stomach bug . . . bronchitis . . . what's the difference?" asked Gretchen.

"The difference it makes is that Blythe said she was there that night because she heard Julie Ann scream."

Gretchen's smile tightened. "And it's kind of hard to scream with bronchitis."

"Not only bronchitis. When I rechecked my notes from Deborah Wood and Sheri Barker, the friends who were with Julie Ann that night, they both said the reason Julie Ann wanted to go home after the movie was because she'd coughed the whole time and could barely speak because of her sore throat and laryngitis."

"So, that's the deep, dark lie that's been perpetuated all these years?"

Coqui nodded, shaking off the drowsiness. "You know better."

Gretchen's face flamed.

"See, once I began uncovering small inconsistencies, I felt maybe Earlene was not the murderer – she was trading her life to protect someone else."

"But not Julie Ann," said Gretchen.

Gretchen's face was fading in and out of focus as Coqui explained, "And it wasn't self-defense – it was premeditated murder."

Gretchen stood and walked to the chair, placing her face inches from Coqui's face as she whispered. "And who is the murderer?"

"Miss Brenda," Coqui slurred.

"And why on God's green Earth would Miss Brenda murder Dexter Sterling?" demanded Gretchen.

But Coqui couldn't answer because a new question was forming in her mind. "How did you know I had a head injury?"

Those were Coqui's last words as everything dissolved into blackness.

Chapter Eighteen

When Coqui awoke, she was tucked neatly into bed. She slowly raised the upper half of her body. Finger by finger, toe by toe, and limb by limb, she did an assessment for any damage. Apparently, no new injuries, but pains from her night in the storage unit flooded unchecked. Everything was intact and she wasn't restrained. Other than deep exhaustion and a thick, cloudy feeling in her head, she was no worse for the wear. Gretchen had obviously drugged her, but not injured her in any other way.

Coqui tried to stand, but she immediately fell back onto the bed. She steadied herself and surveyed her surroundings. Her best guess: she was in one of the residents' rooms at Knollwood Village. Her eyes frantically searched the room – her tote was nowhere in sight. Her shoulders slumped; her head began throbbing. She squeezed her eyes shut. If she made it out of this alive, Mateo would kill her for sure.

Before she began weighing her options, the door eased open and Gretchen walked in. "Good afternoon," Then she checked her watch. "Or, I guess I should say 'Good evening.'"

Coqui sighed. "I'm so stupid."

"Foolish? Yes." Gretchen smiled. "But certainly not stupid – just the reverse. You are very clever . . . and persistent."

"How are you going to conveniently explain away my murder?" asked Coqui.

"Oh, no, Coqui." There was a genuine look of apology on Gretchen's face. "If I had wanted you dead, you'd already be gone. Just a nice cup of coffee with a heavy dose of sleeping pills served my purpose."

"So, what do you want from me?" asked Coqui.

"What we've always wanted from you – drop the case," said Gretchen.

"And if I don't?" persisted Coqui. She said it with more resolve than she felt.

"Then so be it – the truth comes out . . . your call." Gretchen sighed. "But before you make your decision, let's both put all our cards on the table. You go first and tell me what you think you've uncovered, and then I'll fill in all your blanks. After all, isn't that why you came down to Hampton today?"

"That's it?" questioned Coqui. "That's all you want?"

"That's all we've ever wanted."

Coqui took in Gretchen's intense gaze. Could she trust this woman?

"That's it. You've been so diligent, you deserve to know everything," said Gretchen.

"And after that?"

"I'll give you back your things, and I'll drive you over to Cooter's where you began your search a week ago. You can call that nice man who has been frantically calling everyone in Hampton this afternoon."

"Mateo," said Coqui.

"Mateo," repeated Gretchen.

"How far did I get before I passed out?" asked Coqui.

"You asked me how I knew about your head injury." She grimaced. "Sorry about that. I only meant to scare you, not harm you."

"Thanks," Coqui croaked.

Coqui tried to order her thoughts. "I went through Earlene's photo albums, and she had all her pictures in order, year by year, each event labeled. She began with all the early pictures with her and Blythe as girls. Then there were several pages of them with Jack and Ricky. All the pictures were in black and white, but I did notice how tiny Earlene was and that Jack wasn't much bigger than she was."

"And then you have Julie Ann and you thought how unusual two such small people would have such a tall child," said Gretchen.

Coqui nodded. "But I dismissed the thought very quickly. After many generations, genes that have been hidden away seem to pop up out of nowhere. So, I searched the Hampton High 1974-75 yearbook and saw a color picture of Jack and Earlene as Homecoming King and Queen. They had on pale blue outfits that matched their eyes."

"Yes," confirmed Gretchen. A soft, wistful smile lit her face. "They both had beautiful, crystal clear blue eyes."

"And it is genetically impossible for two blue-eyed people to produce a brown-eyed child." Coqui paused and looked at Gretchen full face. "But even then, I didn't see the whole story. I thought that maybe Julie Ann wasn't Jack Thornton's child. But Earlene seemed absolutely devoted to Jack – according to everyone I spoke to. It wasn't until later that I began wondering if, in fact, was Julie Ann Earlene's daughter."

"Go on," said Gretchen.

"Earlene had definitely been pregnant, and as kind as Brenda was to everyone, she seemed especially dedicated to Julie Ann. I felt the need to search deeper into Brenda Watkins relationship and interest in Earlene and her baby."

Gretchen nodded.

"Like I said, part of my search led me to the Hampton High School yearbooks. I went back to the first year Miss Brenda became a teacher and followed her through the years she taught until Earlene's graduating class – 1975. There was a faculty picture for Brenda Watkins every year except for 1975-1976. Then, she returned the following year and taught until the 1988-89 school year. I thought of reasons for someone to take a year off. She could have decided to travel, go to graduate school . . . maybe an illness on her part. That's when I called you and you said that she'd been sent to care for her father's sister who'd been in an automobile accident."

"And you don't think she did?"

"No," said Coqui. "When I reviewed my notes with my conversation with Deborah Woods, she told me that like Brenda, her dad had been an only child."

"You are thorough."

"There is another good reason to disappear . . . " Coqui nodded her head slowly. "Maybe Brenda got pregnant and stayed out of sight for that period of time."

"See, I told you that you aren't stupid."

"Being an unwed mother would have been scandalous at the time – especially for such a well-thought of family like the Watkins."

"And that would mean Julie Ann's mama is really Brenda Watkins," said Gretchen.

"Is she?" asked Coqui.

"You're right," confirmed Gretchen. "Brenda Watkins is Julie Ann's biological mother. By agreement, both Earlene and Brenda wanted it to stay a secret."

"What happened to Earlene's baby?" asked Coqui.

"Let me back up a bit. Brenda Watkins found out she was pregnant the summer of 1975, the summer Earlene married Jack and Blythe married Ricky. The Watkins were a high-profile family in Hampton, as you already know, and they were proud of their strict morals. An abortion was out of the question, and raising an illegitimate child was not an option either. So, Brenda remained confined at home, but the word was she'd gone to care for an elderly relative."

"And everyone believed that?" asked Coqui.

Gretchen smiled. "Like most towns, large and small, facts begin to change as they ride down the information highway, but by and large, I think everyone accepted that. The Watkins arranged with their private physician to check in on Miss Brenda, and when her time came, to deliver the baby at a nearby clinic."

"I'm surprised they didn't insist she have the baby at home," said Coqui.

"The Watkins were practical people and wanted to ensure that if something did go wrong, there'd be proper resources nearby. After the birth, the baby would be placed in a good home."

"But how did Earlene become involved?" asked Coqui. She now knew this part of the story from her conversation with Cindy Sullivan. The other patient who came in that night was not Mr. Watkins, but his daughter. It was her doctor who'd sent Cindy home, none the wiser. But she wanted Gretchen to supply these details, to see how honest she was really being.

Gretchen resumed her story. "Earlene took Jack's death hard. Blythe stayed with her constantly. The two had always been close cousins, and young widowhood brought them even closer. One night Earlene went into premature labor. Blythe put her in the car with the intention of driving her to the hospital, but soon it was evident they weren't going to make it. Luck... fate . . . call it what you will, they passed by the clinic."

"And Blythe took her in, and Brenda came in hours later for her delivery," said Coqui.

Gretchen nodded. "Earlene's baby died and Brenda's baby needed a home. Both were agreeable, so other than Earlene, Blythe, Brenda, and the doctor, no one was the wiser."

"Did Brenda ever say who the father was?" asked Coqui.

"No, not even the father knew," confirmed Gretchen.

Everything jelled into a complete picture. Now Coqui understood. "Until one week before his death."

Chapter Nineteen

"Dexter Sterling," confirmed Gretchen. "You see, the woman who was the nurse on duty that night moved to Florida, and years later became involved with Dexter."

"I know," confessed Coqui. "I've been in touch with her."

"Cindy Sullivan had no idea of what transpired that evening at the clinic. One night when she and Dexter had had too much to drink, they were sharing stories about people in Hampton." Gretchen sighed. "Without even realizing the set of events she would be setting in motion, she told Dexter about the night at the clinic. Apparently, on her way to her car that night, she saw the Watkins' car, but never figured out that it was a baby that brought them to the clinic. Mr. Watkins had heart issues." Gretchen shrugged. "Cindy must have thought it was something to do with him."

"And Dexter put two and two together and saw an opportunity to set himself up for life," said Coqui.

"I was surprised that Dexter was that smart –'

"He wasn't," interrupted Coqui. "He and Cindy had looked at Hampton High School yearbooks the night before he left. He noticed the same thing I did . . . the color Homecoming picture of the blue-eyed king and queen."

Gretchen nodded. "Whatever he thought, we'll never know. But, one thing we do know is he was a gambler and he longed for the good life."

"The easy, good life," corrected Coqui.

"And what better than blackmail?"

"And he must have smelled something fishy," said Coqui. "He headed straight to Hampton. He must have figured that if his hunch was right, Earlene would be an easy target to give up the information he hoped to get."

"The perfect opportunity for blackmail," said Gretchen as she nodded. "As usual, Dexter couldn't help himself and he called Earlene to tell her he was on his way back and what he suspected. She must have confessed. Dexter told Earlene she should tell Brenda to have her first payment ready for him when he got there."

"So, it *was* premeditated?" confirmed Coqui.

"Brenda was at the trailer waiting for Dexter when he got there, and she had brought a gun."

"So, the gun was Brenda Watkins's gun?" interrupted Coqui.

Gretchen shook her head and smiled. "The gun Earlene was holding was Miss Brenda's gun, but the gun that shot and killed Dexter was Earlene's."

"But Earlene and Brenda hadn't planned on Julie Ann's early return," said Coqui as the final pieces began to slide into place.

"Julie Ann was so focused on the quarrel that she headed straight for the ruckus. But when Julie Ann came in, total chaos broke loose. In a way, it was fortunate she blacked out, so they could come up with an alternate scenario."

"What was the plan supposed to be?" she asked.

"Earlene had a gun registered to her name. She'd had it for years. Miss Brenda made her get it once Dexter had beaten her up. That night, when Dexter arrived, he would be expecting to see Earlene and Miss Brenda. The plan was for Earlene to have Miss Brenda's gun in her hand when Dexter came in. She would get his attention and then maneuver him around so that he would be facing the closet where Miss Brenda was hiding. When he was in position, Miss Brenda would come out of the closet and fire Earlene's gun to kill Dexter. Afterward, they would switch guns, replacing Miss Brenda's fingerprints with Earlene's."

"But why?' Coqui raised her hand. "Why would Miss Brenda shoot him?"

"Miss Brenda had been raised around guns all her life. She was an expert marksman." Gretchen smiled sadly. "Plus, that was Miss Brenda for you. She didn't want to put that hardship on Earlene. She would have done anything for her." Gretchen readjusted her position. "Once he was dead, they'd set up a scene where it looked like Earlene had shot him in self-defense. Miss Brenda would leave. Earlene would call Chief Holbrook, and no one would question their story . . . no witnesses."

"And no one would have bothered to differ," said Coqui. "That would also explain Julie Ann's strange statement."

"Strange statement?" asked Gretchen. "What did she say?"

"That Dexter seemed startled . . . distracted right before he pushed her down."

"That must have been when Miss Brenda came out of the closet," said Gretchen. "Julie Ann wouldn't have known she was there."

Coqui nodded. "And Julie Ann fell to the ground, hit her head, and blacked out. And that's when Miss Brenda raised the gun and fired at Dexter."

"Julie Ann coming home turned everything upside down," said Gretchen. "With everything happening in chaos, they had to quickly come up with another plan."

Coqui looked at Gretchen. "And how do you know the details so well?"

"My dad drove Miss Brenda to the trailer that night. He was in on everything," said Gretchen. "As I said, we all owe a lot to Miss Brenda. She's a good woman. Her being locked up in jail for the rest of her life just didn't seem to be the best choice. Earlene gave up so much for Julie Ann to have a better life." Gretchen returned Coqui's intense gaze.

"So, how are you going to answer the question, 'Did Julie Ann's mother murder Dexter Sterling?'"

Gretchen stood and walked to the door. She stopped and turned slightly around, looking over her shoulder. "This new information gives a strange twist to the answer for that question."

Coqui didn't speak for a few minutes, just staring into Gretchen's eyes. Giving a slight sigh, she said, "And now it's my turn to see how justice can best be served."

Chapter Twenty

Cooter's Ruff 'n Tumble was just as packed as it had been last Saturday night, the first time Coqui had met Blythe Rawlins . . . unbelievable that it had only been a week ago. The old woman was settled in at her regular table nursing a beer. Coqui slid in to face her.

Without looking up Blythe said, "Well, now you know everythin'. Don't know why you're here pesterin' me again."

"Well, you know how I hate loose ends," said Coqui. "I'm here to talk. You can just listen if you like." Coqui leaned back. "But feel free to join in if you have anything you'd like to add."

"I thought you were here to meet that feller who's been buggin' everybody in Hampton today." A smirk followed her comment.

"That, too," said Coqui.

Blythe eyed Coqui, turned up the bottle, and then set it down with a clunk. Shrugging her shoulders, she clipped, "Talk away then. I'm not goin' anywhere."

Coqui relaxed into her seat. "I'm assuming Gretchen called you." Coqui's mouth tugged downward. "And yeah, I did piece a lot of it together . . . and with what Gretchen told me, I guess I know just about everything; and, it now makes a lot more sense."

"Amazin'," snorted Blythe. "Will wonders never cease?"

"Some parts of this story just didn't add up while other parts too easily fell into place to make it work." Coqui paused. "So, I came here today to uncover the rest of the story. And I got those pieces from Gretchen . . . but you already know that."

Blythe's expression gave nothing away.

"Julie Ann never found out that Miss Brenda was her real mom?" asked Coqui.

"Earlene is Julie Ann's real mama!" Blythe fired back.

"You're right. Earlene loved Julie Ann – brought her home from the clinic, stayed up with her at nights when she was sick. Kissed boo-boos and patched up scraped knees. Helped her with school projects. Gave her a shoulder to cry on when some boy broke her heart. Miss Brenda provided a body for her to develop and money for her material needs. Both important roles, but Earlene was her real mama." Coqui shifted in her seat. "Let's leave that for now."

Blythe grunted and rolled her eyes.

"And in return, Miss Brenda had Julie Ann at her doorstep, able to watch her grow up and have a relationship with her that wouldn't have been possible if the baby had been sent away." Coqui paused. "Everything worked out as best as possible for all concerned. Julie Ann didn't have a dad, but she had three loving people who genuinely cared for her welfare – Earlene, Miss Brenda, and you, Blythe."

"But then walks in Mr. Wonderful hisself." Blythe stared into her beer. "Sometimes you just can't get rid of a disease."

Coqui leaned inward. "And that, Mrs. Rawlins, is very true. People like Dexter seem to get away with way too much. But you aren't the one to judge." As Coqui herself had learned over the last few days.

"Don't talk down to me, missy!" Blythe cocked her head. "I didn't like you from the minute I met you. I knew you'd be trouble. Miss Fancy pants comin' down to straighten out us hicks."

"And I didn't like you either," returned Coqui, her face flaming. "And I still don't." She reached into her tote and pulled out the colored photo of Earlene and Jack as Homecoming King and Queen that she'd printed that morning. "But I do admire your loyalty to Earlene." She handed the picture to Blythe.

The old woman's jaw tightened, her eyes brimming with tears. She brought the picture closer. "Earlene never hurt nobody."

"No, she didn't."

She straightened her shoulders, the old cockiness returning. She tossed the photo in Coqui's face. "Ball's in your court now." She held up her hand. "Another beer," Blythe called out to the waitress.

"Gretchen said the same thing."

All was quiet save for the beginning swell of chatter from the after-work crowd.

Blythe's face went slack. "Nobody's goin' to stop you." Her voice softened. "But what would be the purpose? Would justice really be served?" She knuckled away the tears streaming down her checks with a gnarly fist. "Dexter was greedy . . . would always have wanted more. Miss Brenda had to stop him."

"While Julie Ann was knocked out," said Coqui. "Miss Brenda shot Dexter point-blank."

Blythe stared at her hands as Coqui continued talking.

"Earlene and Miss Brenda had to come up with a whole new chain of events."

"Why do you keeping rehashin' everythin'?" screamed Blythe. "Miss Brenda had to do something – Dexter was scum!"

Coqui shook her head. "But the minute any lawyer brought out all the sordid details, Miss Brenda would have been charged with premeditated murder."

"Earlene didn't want an investigation," said Blythe.

"I understand why neither would want an investigation," said Coqui.

"So, that's when they called me over and we decided what to do. The first thing was to get Miss Brenda out of there."

"Because it might have come out that Julie Ann was Brenda Watkins and Dexter Sterling's child, not Earlene and Jack's."

Blythe nodded. "Earlene's life had been a disaster . . . but Julie Ann had a chance for a better one."

"And Ms. Watkins took care of everything," said Coqui.

"Chief Holbrook never knew the difference . . . never wanted to know the truth," inserted Blythe.

"But in the end, it was Earlene who had to pay the price," finished Coqui.

"They all deserved better," spat Blythe.

"You're right. They deserved a lot better," agreed Coqui.

Blythe straightened, holding her shoulders erect. "So, Miss Private Investigator, what do you plan to do?" she asked.

Coqui sighed. "Tell Julie Ann her mama's story was the only story I could find."

"It's a sad story," said Blythe.

"And I don't need to make it any sadder."

Blythe stared over Coqui's shoulder. "Looks like your feller is here to fetch you."

Coqui turned around and caught Mateo's attention, signaling him she's be there in a minute.

Mateo waved back, and he didn't look any too happy.

"He's a cute 'un." Blythe winked.

Coqui stood and peered down. "You're right about two things, Mrs. Rawlins." She looked over her shoulder at Mateo once again, and then she returned her attention to the old woman and leaned inches from her face. "He is a cute 'un." Then Coqui straightened and smiled. "And, sometimes it *is* best to let sleeping dogs lie." Then she slid Earlene and Jack's Homecoming photo back across the table to Blythe.

The End

Also by Janice Alonso

That's the Spirit!
Do Not Be Afraid
Make a Joy-filled Noise
Mary's Song
The Secret to Receiving Pure Joy
Love in the Time of Covid
Thy Will Be Done
God's Handiwork
Let There Be Light
The Jesus Man
Failure Is Not Fatal
What's in a Name?
Embrace the Good
Keeping the Faith
All in a Day's Work
"X" Marks the Spot
Welcome
An Easter Discovery
A Picture Is Worth a Thousand Words
Quilting for God
A New Creation
What a Difference a Year Makes
My Cup Overflows
Don't Overlook the Little Things
Vessels of Beauty
Same Story Told in a New Way
God's Morning Messenger
Up Close and Personal
Ever-changing Nature; Never-changing God
No Job Too Small
Defined by the Holy Spirit
Free at Last
Unexpected Paths

Literary Short Stories
The Final Chapter - A Short Story Collection

Love God. Love Me.
Too Little or Too Big?
I Wish . . .
Everyone Has Something to Give
Where's Lucy Ladybug?
Many Second Chances

Love God. Love Others.
Just the Same in Different Ways
I Don't Want to Go to a Princess Party
The Little Circus Lion
Enough Love for Everyone
You Don't Have a Home?
Miss Bossy Pants
No Means No
New Places, New Faces
You're Not Invited
A Jealous Heart

Murder Most Mysterious
Let Sleeping Dogs Lie
Murder Most Mysterious - Death Has Pouty Red Lips

Standalone
The Snowsantas Find the Christmas Spirit

Watch for more at janicealonso.com.

About the Author

Janice Alonso's work appears regularly in Christian, mystery, and children's publications.

Read more at janicealonso.com.

www.ingramcontent.com/pod-product-compliance
Lightning Source LLC
Chambersburg PA
CBHW020321170225
21954CB00001B/37